Once Again

By

Amy Durham

DEDICATION

To Jayne Squires, who first told me I could do this and whose belief in me translated into my belief in myself.

CONTENTS

Once Again

ACKNOWLEDGMENTS

Teresa Reasor, I can never thank you enough for your support, encouragement, and expertise. For reading and critiquing for me, I give you my deepest gratitude. To Kari Lee Townsend, thank you for your insightful editing and critiquing, for believing in this book, and for helping me make it even better. To my fellow KY Romance Writer members, thank you for the wonderful camaraderie that exists only between fellow writers. To Glenda Edwards, thanks for 25 years of abiding friendship and all the encouragement and brainstorming a girl could want. To Ray Hollenbach and the rest of the folks in my local writers group, thank you for your encouragement and for giving me a place to share this part of myself. To my parents, every opportunity I've ever had has been because of you. No words are sufficient, but thank you nonetheless. To my husband, Kevin, thank you for loving the creative side of me (and the rest of me!) unconditionally. Kelly, my first-born, thank you for believing in my dreams – I hope my ambitions will inspire your own. To Eli and Reece, thank you for the infinite joy you bring me. And most importantly, thank you God for imagination, creativity, and storytelling, and for putting all of the above in me.

PROLOGUE

Okay, I had to admit that Maine in July was spectacular.

Spotless white clouds dotted a sky of perfect aqua blue. Bright green leaves hung heavy in the trees. Together with the rich landscaping of the town, nature had created a lovely and charming little place.

My parents had chosen an extraordinary location for our new home.

But, being sixteen, I didn't say it out loud. I was still pretty unhappy about leaving Nashville. Music City, USA had been my one and only home, and the thought of starting over with only two years of high school left scared me silly.

Not that I'd been at the top of the social ladder in Nashville. Far from it. But I'd been me, and I'd known where I stood. Now, who knew what or where I'd end up?

It seemed odd to spend Independence Day house-hunting in Sky Cove, Maine, but my parents had decided July fourth would be the perfect time to visit before making the move. After touring several places, we'd settled on a red-brick house in a middle-class neighborhood. Two-floors, it was a perfect square rising up from the ground, very much like a cracker box. In addition to some storage space, the small upstairs had one bedroom and one bathroom, and my parents had agreed it could be mine.

It was a perk meant to make me happy. To ease the transition.

It sort of did. I liked the idea of having the second floor to myself.

Heading across town to the realtor's office to settle the business of purchasing the new home, my parents took the road that ran parallel to the ocean. I lounged in the backseat, watching the gaps in the trees lining the road as they gave me glimpses of the shore just beyond. The blue of the water surprised me when I first saw it. Somehow I'd thought it would be green and brown and ugly.

The bits of shore I could see were rough and rocky, with patches of sand scattered throughout. I thought how nice it must be to walk barefoot on the sandy spots on warm summer days.

At once, I felt a huge longing to walk the beach, combined with a strange sense of foreboding. The air in the car turned damp, and liquid seemed to fill my lungs with each breath. The temperature dropped, far too cold for July.

Disconcerted, I turned around for one last look at the shore before we headed into the town. An opening in the trees offered an unobstructed view, and I saw a woman jogging.

No, that wasn't right. She was running. And she was wearing a dress. A really old looking dress. How odd.

A family picnicking on the beach sat directly in her path, yet she didn't slow. She just kept running. She didn't even seem to see them in front of her.

My heart picked up speed. I craned my neck and turned in my seat, the aged vinyl upholstery creaking as I shifted. Knowing the collision was imminent, I held my breath. The running woman plowed right into the family eating happily on their blanket.

I cringed.

Then realized that nothing had happened.

Mystery woman still ran down the beach with frantic speed, but the family still sat, enjoying their holiday picnic.

I squinted. She kept running toward a rock wall, and the forward momentum of our car took me further away. Her form grew smaller and... transparent?

No, of course not.

And then she disappeared, like dust blowing away in the breeze.

My skin warmed as the cold air in the car faded.

I rubbed my eyes, shook my head, and turned back to face the front of the car. It had been a very long day.

CHAPTER ONE

The morning fog that swirled through Sky Cove had lifted. The sun warmed the air, and it was a lovely late-August day.

I'd convinced Mom not to drive me to school on my first morning.

On the day that I, Layla Bradford, started my junior year of high school in a strange and far-off place.

Well, maybe Sky Cove wasn't exactly *that* far-off, but compared to Nashville, it might as well have been the other side of the universe.

Truth be told, the town was kind of nice. And the summer weather was spectacular. I'd been surprised to learn that gray and overcast wasn't the norm for Maine. The sun apparently knew how to shine here as well as it did in Tennessee.

Yep, Sky Cove was lovely.

But it wasn't the city. No crazy traffic. No shopping malls. Not that a shopping mall was ever a huge draw for me, but I did enjoy the bookstores. And I was pretty sure that the pleasant summer weather I'd been enjoying since my arrival two weeks ago would soon turn to a winter like I'd never seen before.

Great. I couldn't wait.

The thing about being a teenager is that you're at the mercy of your parents' decisions. Mine decided to move to Maine, and despite the fact that it was about the last thing in the world I wanted, I didn't have it in me to be one of those bratty, whiny kids who made their parents miserable when everything wasn't going their way. Besides, I could see how excited my dad was about String City, the guitar store he now owned.

So... here I was.

Pulling my old, sensible Honda into the parking lot of Sky Cove Senior High School.

I'd worn my favorite baby-doll shirt, the teal green one. My mom said it matched the color of my eyes. I guess moms are supposed to say stuff like that, but the shirt did lend me a little confidence in my appearance. And because the breeze in a coastal town forever whooshed about in the mornings, I'd left the natural waves in my shoulder length brown hair. No sense spending all that time with a flat iron if the wind was just going to whip it around.

Another thing about this town is that, with a population of less than five thousand, there's only one high school. Which means everyone knows everybody and there are no secrets.

Or so I've been told about small towns.

At any rate, I knew finding a way to fit in would be difficult. Most of these kids had grown up here and been in the same classes since nursery school.

Fitting in had never been my number one priority. No, I was always more of a *blending* in kind of girl. I didn't try to be noticed by having the right friends or dressing the *correct* way. I just wanted to fly under the radar.

I hated being the center of attention.

Which was exactly what I became the moment I stepped through the front door of the school.

My mom and I had toured the school with the principal last week, which was helpful, because I already knew where my classes were and wouldn't have to stumble my way through the first day. But what I hadn't realized was that the front lobby was the *gathering spot*.

Kids sat in chairs, the floor, and leaned up against the walls. Every face turned and every eye focused on me as I walked in. I'd avoided, on purpose, arriving at school early, to steer clear of just this thing. They all stared, and I knew they were sizing me up, deciding whether or not I was worthy, and ultimately finding me lacking in the wow-she's-hot department.

My silent plea for rescue was answered when the warning bell rang, sending students scattering on their way to homerooms.

Squaring my shoulders, I took a deep breath and turned toward my hallway. The school building had seen better days – probably in the 1960s – and the painted cinderblock walls and dingy gray tile floors held the scents of aged textbooks, the odd, generic odor of a school cafeteria, and the more recent smell of endless mists of body spray.

My homeroom was the third door on the right. A few students still loitered by the hall entrance, so I smiled as I walked past. One boy greeted me with a nod of his head that I was sure he believed to be very suave and cool. He wasn't much taller than me, and I was five-three. Another guy, this one average height, looked at me with guarded, narrowed eyes, as if trying to figure out who I was. Two girls, clearly cheerleaders with their school-spirit shirts and ponytails tied with matching bows, looked at me with judgment in their eyes.

I sighed inwardly. Some things were the same no matter where you lived.

Behind the others was a taller boy, with dark blond hair, a deep golden that picked up the dreary fluorescent lights from the lobby and turned them into something special.

A zing of awareness barreled into me, an uneasy combination of both *rightness* and menace settling heavy in my stomach, and I had the strangest sensation that I'd felt exactly this way before.

Unlike some of the other guys I'd seen during that brief moment of panic in the crowded lobby, Mr. Dark Blond didn't look like a slob. His green polo shirt was tucked into his jeans, and he wore a belt.

Of course, he had the kind of body that looked good with a tucked in shirt and belt accentuating his waist. Long, tall, and lean. And though I'd never considered myself a superficial, all-about-appearances person, I was girl enough to notice.

In the split second that I passed by him, all sorts of thoughts bounced around in my brain about how to acknowledge him. I'd smiled at the group, after all, and even nodded back to the shorter boy who'd wowed me with his head-nod. I couldn't just ignore the cute one, could I?

But at the same time, I couldn't make too big of a deal about him either.

I looked up at him, figuring some brief eye contact and a generic smile would do the trick.

But when my eyes met his, it was to find him already looking at me. Staring really, like he'd seen a ghost. Eyes wide. Mouth open slightly as if he wanted to say something but didn't know what. The intensity was almost uncomfortable. And his eyes were crazy beautiful, deep and brown.

Did I have something on my face? Toilet paper stuck to my shoe?

Because really, there was no way he was actually noticing me. Not with the two Barbie dolls hanging all over him. I was not the kind of girl who attracted attention from boys like him.

And besides, he looked like he couldn't decide whether or not to be happy about my presence.

But his stare continued, so I half-smiled at him, kind of apologetically, and with a shrug pushed my way into the hallway and found my homeroom.

***

My first class was chemistry, and the scent of hot Bunsen burners and what they'd once heated filled the room. This class was not going to be my favorite. I'd been indifferent about my biology class last year, and had gotten through it, managing to maintain my grade point average. But I had a feeling that chemistry was going to be a struggle.

Fortunately for me, I didn't have a social life that got in the way of my study habits.

And also fortunately for me, I ended up paired with a science nut for a lab partner. Her name was Jessie Spencer, and she was actually really nice.

She seemed to be like me, an under-the-radar type.

I suppose you could say she was my first friend.

"I've never been further south that Boston," she told me as the bell rang to end first period. "I bet Tennessee is really awesome."

"I liked it a lot," I answered. "But I lived there all my life, so I probably took it for granted."

"You miss it, I'm sure." She grabbed her books and headed for the door, her chin-length curly brown hair bobbing with every step.

Sure I did. But I wasn't going to dwell on it.

"Some." I picked up my backpack and walked into the hallway with her. "It's hard starting over, but Sky Cove is really beautiful."

It turned out Jessie's locker was only three doors down from mine, and while we picked up books for our second period classes, she introduced me to two of her friends.

"Hey, this is Layla Bradford. She's new here." Since Jessie had been so kind to me this morning, I decided not to deduct points for stating the obvious.

"And these are my friends, Marsha Foster and Tiffany Caldwell." She turned back to me. "Tomorrow after school we're going to the beach. You should come."

I told her I'd think about it, and said a quick hello to Marsha and Tiffany. We left moments later, as we all had classes to go to, but I had to admit Marsha and Tiffany had been just as kind and welcoming as Jessie. It seemed the three of them were just like I'd always been, middle-class citizens in the caste-system that was public high school.

Which was fine. It was a status quo I was familiar with.

A shiver of sensation danced up my spine as I left the row of lockers to find my next class. Looking around, I made certain no one was staring at me, then did a quick check of my appearance. My pants were not unzipped, bra strap was not showing. Short of mascara running down my face, it seemed nothing was wrong with the way I looked.

But I couldn't shake the feeling of being watched. The disturbing sense of unease returned full force.

Somewhere in my mind words bounced and ricocheted, and at the door to my classroom I stopped and closed my eyes.

Behind my eyelids a sentence began to take shape. Each word falling into place, like slot machine wheels, until I saw it clearly.

I won't lose. Not this time.

Opening my eyes I took a deep breath to clear my head. How weird was that? What the heck did that mean? I chalked it up to the stress of starting a new school.

The hallway bustled with movement as kids rushed to second period. A sea of unknown faces washed passed me.

I must've been more nervous than I thought.

I squared my shoulders and stepped in to the classroom. Literature class. It wasn't a required course, but rather one of the "elective" classes that I got to choose. So, of course, I chose something that involved reading.

I expected to see other bookworms in the room, and to some degree I wasn't surprised. When I stepped through the door, I noticed three kids sitting quietly with books already out and opened. I smiled. Others like me, who read not because they were forced, but because they enjoyed. Near the front of the room were three girls with cell phones out, frantically sending text messages before the warning bell rang. I wondered if they were in this class because they signed up late and all the other electives were full.

Just as I was about to take a seat with the bookworms, I noticed him.

Him.

Mr. Dark Blond and Brown-Eyed.

On the far side of the room, with one of two empty seats in the class right next to him.

When I looked at him, his eyes narrowed, in a way that seemed familiar and very unsettling, and reached over to remove his books from the unoccupied desk beside him. He dropped his eyes from me to the now empty desk and back again, like some sort of silent invitation.

And did he expect me to just sit there because he said to?

I was pretty certain that was how most girls reacted to him, so why should he think I'd be any different?

Well, I was different, and I was going to prove it by going over and taking the other empty seat with the bookworms.

But when I took a step, it was toward him. Despite the argument in my head, my feet took me in his direction until I was sitting in the very seat he'd cleared for me.

When had I become so weak?

I dropped my backpack on the floor, and stared at it, wondering what in the world I was supposed to say.

"I'm Lucas."

Man, his voice was nice. Deep and mature, there was no hint of the cracking and squeaking of many guys my age. Nope, this was the voice of a boy solidly on the other side of puberty. Smooth and dark, like melted caramel.

"Hi," I said, angry with myself for sounding sheepish, even to my own ears. "Layla."

He nodded and leaned toward me, the wariness in his expression still present. He tilted his head, as if he needed a closer look. "Nice to meet you Layla."

I knew I was blushing. I hated that. I could feel the heat creeping into my cheeks as his eyes scanned back and forth across my face. It made responding verbally to his compliment almost impossible.

I managed a muttered "thanks", just as the warning bell rang and the teacher, Mrs. Chadwick, started class.

I glanced at Lucas once more, as Mrs. Chadwick took attendance, and found him looking at me with an expression that same expression… oddly curious, knowing. I couldn't look away. And when he made no move to say anything, I broke the staring contest by opening my notebook.

Forty-seven minutes later, the bell to end class rang. The texters from the front of the class immediately went for their cells. Rolling my eyes, I reached toward the floor for my backpack, and my hand brushed Lucas's as he bent to pick up his.

Electricity streaked through my arm, and I barely resisted the urge to wrench my hand away. Lucas's eyes met mine, and though I felt certain he hadn't felt the same punch I did, I was pretty sure my face was plastered with shock.

How embarrassing.

"Why are they even in this class?" I nodded toward the girls with the cell phones, hoping my question would put a stop to the awkward moment.

"They probably got stuck here when the other electives filled up." He shrugged and grinned. Not only was it the first pleasant look I'd gotten from him, but his smile was a total killer. "Not a lot of kids choose to take a class where you have to read books."

But apparently he did. Which was both a selling point and a mystery.

We stepped into the hallway at the same time, and before taking off, he looked back at me as if he wanted to say something. In that moment of hesitation before he spoke, the words began falling again, faster this time.

I stood, rooted to my spot. From the end of the hall someone called his name, and Lucas turned to join them.

Paralyzed, I didn't move as the words fell into place.

No matter what I have to do.

CHAPTER TWO

Though I tried not to, I worried about lunch all through the next two periods. I should've asked my new friend Jessie what time her lunch break was, but being overwhelmed with everything, I hadn't thought about it. As a result, U.S. History, which under normal circumstances I would've enjoyed, was a blur, and the geometry class had seemed much more difficult to endure than it would have otherwise.

What if I had nowhere to sit and no one to talk to?

I imagined the worst-case scenario. Standing in the cafeteria, lunch tray in hand, looking at a room of full tables, the occupants staring back at me with no hint of invitation in their eyes.

So I breathed a sigh of relief when I saw Jessie, along with Marsha and Tiffany, waving to me from a table in the center of the cafeteria.

The banana was the best part of lunch, as the turkey sandwich was pretty dry and the steamed broccoli was mostly tasteless, but I did meet a few other people at lunch. A couple of boys at our table seemed overly attentive, as if jockeying for position on the new girl's priority list. They were decent guys, and I was pretty sure they didn't often get the opportunity to try and impress girls. I felt bad, in a way, that they didn't make an enormous impression, but I couldn't recall any names by the end of the day.

Walking to my car, I thought to myself that as far as first days at a new school went, this one hadn't been completely terrible. It was also worth noting that a late-August afternoon in Nashville, Tennessee would've most likely been sweltering. But here in Sky Cove it was warm without humidity, and the breeze was almost balmy as it lifted my hair off my shoulders.

Groups of kids were gathered at various locations in the parking lot. The traditional end-of-the-day debriefing I figured. I was almost to my car when one group of particularly athletic looking boys called my name.

I stopped, looked over my shoulder. I recognized none of them. Apparently they'd heard about me.

"Hey Layla!" the one with the short brown hair yelled.

I just stood there, unsure of how to respond. I didn't even know their names.

"Lay-la," he said again, putting the emphasis on the first syllable.

Great.

The other guys snickered. A slight crowd started to pile up.

"Lay Lay Lay-la," he went on.

I began to hope the ground would open up and engulf me.

"Lay-la, why don't you come over here and lay this." A not-so-subtle pelvic thrust accompanied the last word.

I felt like a statue, and a complete idiot, rooted to the pavement, unable to move. I shook my head and rolled my eyes in disgust, thinking it would be best to just head to my car and ignore the display of ignorance. Even though a part of me – a part that never, ever found the nerve to come out – wanted to let loose with a series of stinging insults, all of which would be way above this moron's vocabulary level.

"Shut up Miller!" came an angry voice from behind me.

And then *he* was there.

Shoving the idiot named Miller hard in the chest.

Miller stumbled back a few steps, looking stunned that Lucas had pushed him.

"Whoa, man." He righted himself, then put up a hand in mock surrender. "I was just saying hello to the new girl."

Lucas got right in his face and jammed a finger in Miller's chest.

"What do you think you accomplish by talking to a girl like that?"

"Dude, look," Miller stammered. "I was just kidding around."

"You feel like a big shot when you act like a jerk?" Lucas took a step closer, now nose-to-nose with the idiot.

"Back off, Luke." Apparently Miller-the-idiot found his spine, though I couldn't figure out why he thought that was a good idea.

For whatever reason, Lucas was livid on my behalf.

How in the world had that happened? Since when did cute guys stick up for me, especially when they looked at me with such guardedness?

"I don't think so, Miller." Lucas shoved again, and Miller had the good sense not to retaliate. "You're the one who needs to back off."

"Hey ladies," Lucas said as he spun around to look at some of the girls who had gathered to watch the confrontation. "Any of you want to be talked to like that?"

Most of the girls just looked at each other or stared at their shoes.

But Lucas wasn't finished. He turned back toward Miller.

"Congratulations, you just made yourself look like a pig in front of half the school."

Never in my life had anyone defended me like this. The fact that I'd barely met him made it all the more unbelievable.

The fact that he was freaking gorgeous made it *completely* unbelievable.

Then he turned to me.
"Come on."
And he took my hand and pulled me toward my car.

CHAPTER THREE

Lucas steered me around to the driver's side of my car with a gentle hand on the small of my back. I was both bewildered and exhilarated by the level of familiarity he displayed with me. And really uncomfortable with the fact that everyone in the parking lot was still looking at me.

"How did you know this was my car?" I grimaced. What a lame thing to say after he'd just defended my honor.

"You were headed this way," he answered, taking my backpack off my shoulder and holding it while I fished inside the front pocket for my keys. "And this is the only car in the row I didn't recognize."

Apparently, he'd decided to quit eyeing me suspiciously.

"Um, I should thank you." My hand closed around my keys. "For before." Great, Layla. That sounded so grateful.

He closed his eyes and took a deep breath, as if still trying to calm down.

"Miller's a complete moron."

"There are idiot boys everywhere," I said, unlocking my car doors. "I learned to ignore them a long time ago."

"I'm sure you encountered plenty of jerks in Tennessee." He opened the back door, put my backpack inside, and closed it. "But my mom would kill me if she found out I saw that and didn't step in."

"You know I'm from Tennessee?"

"News travels fast around here," he said. "And I'm really sorry you had to deal with Miller's stupidity on your first day."

"Not your fault. But thanks again."

He leaned against the back door, seeming in no hurry to leave.

"Lucas Ellis, by the way." He extended his hand. "I realized I didn't tell you my last name in lit class this morning."

"Layla Bradford." I put my hand in his, awed by the welcoming feeling that enveloped not only my fingers and palm, but my entire body. The touch of his skin on mine sent excitement coursing through me. A random thought went through my mind – *Hadn't I known it would be this way?* - though I knew it was impossible.

I'd never felt anything like it before in my life.

"Well, Layla Bradford," he said, not releasing my hand just yet. Reaching around me with his free hand, he pulled my door open.

I slid in wordlessly, and looked up at him.

He winked and shut it. "I'll see you tomorrow."

***

My mom made my favorite - fettuccini alfredo - for dinner, in honor of my first day of school. Of course, the conversation in our muted green eat-in kitchen was the anticipated game of twenty thousand questions from my mom and dad about how my day went.

"Did you like your classes?"

"Did you make any friends?"

"How was the cafeteria food?"

I answered as vaguely as I could, without seeming too distracted. The truth was that the first day at Sky Cove Senior High hadn't been all that bad. And the unpleasant encounter with Miller-the-idiot, whose first name I still did not know, had resulted in that amazing exchange with Lucas Ellis.

I couldn't stop thinking about it. About him.

And I wasn't about to talk boys with my parents.

"Cute boys?" Apparently my mom was not on the same page with me.

"A bit early for that, Mom." I twirled a bite of pasta onto my fork and enjoyed the creamy garlic flavor.

"I guess you're right," she said with a grin that reached all the way to deep brown eyes that matched the dark mahogany of her hair.

My mom was great, and I loved her dearly. But Lucas Ellis? I just wasn't ready to talk about him yet. It seemed... I don't know... like he was just mine for the moment.

Crazy, stupid thoughts.

I mentally lectured myself on my stupidity.

"Do you have homework?" Thankfully Mom caught the hint and moved on to another subject.

"Not tonight," I said, taking my empty dishes and rinsing them in the sink. "But I'm sure that will change tomorrow."

"Probably right," Dad put in, bringing his plate to the sink.

My mom and dad were older than most parents of kids my age, evidenced by the gray sprinkled through my dad's black hair, but I liked to think that made them a little less uptight.

"I'm going to get my folders organized and my binder put together tonight," I said as I loaded my dinner dishes in the dishwasher. It was a good excuse to escape to my room for a while.

Mom nodded. She knew my routine. I was a creature of habit. And after a day of school and dinner with my parents, I enjoyed a bit of alone time in my room with my iPod and my thoughts.

And tonight my thoughts were all about Lucas Ellis.

I felt brainless. He was just a boy. And I'd known him all of ten hours.

I decided I'd made too much of the incident this afternoon. It was my emotions getting the better of me. The stress of starting at a new school. The strain of feeling alone and putting on a happy face in spite of it.

I realized, though, that I hadn't felt alone with Lucas. Either in literature class or in the parking lot. I felt... *at home.*

How crazy was that?

I turned on my box fan. I'd been unprepared for the fact that most houses in Maine didn't have air conditioning. Summers were short here, and some houses had window units, but for the most part, people in Sky Cove just made due with fans during July and August.

Having been raised in the south, not having air conditioning was strange. And uncomfortable. Thus, the box fan.

I smiled as the moving air touched me and cooled my warm skin. I plugged my ears with headphones, and flipped to last year's playlist on my iPod. Songs that had been current during the last school year pumped out of the tiny earbuds. I tried to imagine Nashville. Adrienne. My other friends. The places I liked to hang out.

None of it was successful at taking my mind off of Lucas.

It was as if my life in Tennessee was a million years ago and the present was all about him.

I flipped open my phone and fired off a text to Adrienne. *What's up?*

She responded immediately.

OMG! I miss u!

Naturally, the texting continued, but only marginally took my mind off Lucas.

I didn't want to forget Nashville and the life I'd had there. I was a teenager, after all. Wasn't I supposed to wallow in self-pity over the things and people I'd been forced to leave behind? Wasn't I supposed to be miserable in this new place out of respect for my former home.

Yeah, that had never been my style. Self-pity wasn't something I allowed myself. And, unlike some kids my age,

I'd already realized that the world didn't revolve around me one hundred percent of the time.

But right at this moment, I'd have gladly given in to teenage angst and drama if it would make me forget about Lucas Ellis.

I aimed the fan toward my bed and snuggled in, trying in vain not to picture dark blond hair and brown eyes.

Trying not to hear that smooth, caramel voice.

Sometime later, I finally fell asleep. And when I did, he was still on my mind.

CHAPTER FOUR

The next morning, the fog still lingered, thick and heavy, as I drove to school. Jessie was waiting in the parking lot for me when I pulled in. As glad as I was to have company for my inevitable walk into the front lobby, the look on her face told me that news of yesterday afternoon's episode had spread.

"Is it true that Todd Miller was harassing you after school yesterday?" she asked.

So his first name was Todd. Funny, I still only thought of him as Miller-the-idiot.

"I suppose," I grabbed my backpack from the backseat. "He was just being an jerk."

"I heard Lucas Ellis put a stop to it."

I considered how best to respond as we walked toward the building. Clearly, Lucas couldn't expect his involvement to remain a secret. Not with the crowd that witnessed the exchange. But I didn't want to make more of it than there was. High school reputations were a tricky balancing act, and you never knew what was going to tip the scales in one direction. Too much interest in the "new girl" could cause him problems.

I was also working very hard to *not* elevate him to hero status. Trying, but failing miserably.

"He was just being nice," I shrugged.

"Yeah, well," Jessie giggled. "Luke has a reputation of being a nice guy, but I've never heard of him getting into a confrontation like that."

As if I needed another reason to put him on a pedestal.

"Who is Todd Miller anyway?" We'd reached the front door, so I lowered my voice as I pushed it open. "I hadn't even laid eyes on him until yesterday afternoon in the parking lot."

"School jock," Jessie said. "Big star on the football and basketball teams. I suppose that's why so many girls want to date him, even though he's a jerk."

"What about Lucas?" We shouldered through the crowd of people in the lobby, working our way down the hall to the door of our first class. "He looks like he'd be an athlete."

"Luke's a runner. Cross country, track and field. He does 5Ks and stuff like that in the off-season. Trains all the time. I heard he's going to do a marathon this year."

"How old is he?" I asked, trying nonchalantly to scan the hall in search of him.

"He's a senior." The warning bell rang and the lobby began to empty. Jessie and I headed into the classroom and took our seats. "And I heard he's single again."

I should not be interested in this. I should *not*. Yet I couldn't stop the next question from leaving my mouth. "Again?"

"Right." Jessie leaned closer, whispering. "He and Kara Jennings have been on and off over the past year. But I heard they broke up some time over summer break."

My curiosity was put on hold when Mr. Hartley started class, and I decided that was a good thing. The conversation with Jessie had already revealed way too much of my interest in Lucas Ellis.

All through chemistry, I was painfully aware of the minutes ticking by. Every click of a pencil on a desk and every scrape of a chair moving against the floor set my nerves on edge. Though I told myself it was because I disliked the class, I knew it was a lie. I was in a hurry for this period to end because my next class was literature.

With Lucas.

Thankfully, I paid enough attention to get the homework assignment written down in my notebook. As the bell rang, Jessie handed me a slip of paper with her phone number on it, and instructions to call her tonight if I had trouble with it.

Bless Jessie. Both for her fast friendship, and her science expertise.

I went to my locker, trying not to hurry. Rushing through the visit with Marsha and Tiffany and sprinting to my next class would be a colossal show of stupidity. But geez, the five-minute break between classes seemed longer than fifty minutes of chemistry.

I deliberately slowed my steps as I approached my lit class. The bookworms were in the same spots as yesterday, books already out and open. The texting girls were still up front, fingers flying across the keys of their cell phones.

One of them had bathed in a sticky, floral smelling perfume, strong enough to make my eyes water. Sheesh. As if a guy's going to be attracted to you just because you smell like a florist's shop.

And Lucas was again on the far side of the room, clearing his books from the desk beside him when he saw me walk in.

It was easier today to make the walk across the room. I didn't feel like I was being beckoned by a guy used to getting his way with girls. I felt like a boy who for some reason wanted to be kind to me was inviting me.

Good grief. This could be trouble. If I started having delusions of grandeur about a guy two social classes above me, I was doomed to disappointment and embarrassment.

Sliding into the seat next to him, I searched for something witty to say. Small-talk under pressure had never been my forte.

"Hey," I said. "I'm happy to report that I haven't seen Miller-the-idiot this morning."

My words sounded ridiculous. Inane. I should've stopped with "hey". Suddenly the fluorescent lights seemed like heat lamps as I felt my face heat from awkwardness.

"You won't see him down this hall a lot," Lucas chuckled. "He's not much into the advanced courses."

I took that to mean that Miller was either stupid or lazy, or a combination of both.

Lucas continued. "Your dad owns the big music store downtown, right?"

Again, he surprised me with the knowledge he already had about my life. Of course, Sky Cove wasn't a huge metropolis, so he'd probably just heard it around town. It didn't mean he was interested enough to go searching for information about me on his own.

"Right," I answered, reaching in my backpack for my book and the folder I'd labeled for this class. Looking back at him, I couldn't resist a lingering look at his deep brown eyes. Since I was looking straight at him, I figured I better say something else. I decided on my dad's new slogan. "Vintage and new guitars and amps, and everything else you might need to start a rock band."

Actually, my dad was now the owner of String City, a thriving business specializing in guitars, both new and old. Kind of strange to find a booming music store in the middle of small-town Maine, but the place had built a reputation over the years, and people were willing to travel to do business here. The previous owner was a guitarist my dad met in Nashville. He'd been in town often to do studio work, which is how my dad knew him. When he decided to move near his daughter and grandkids in Texas, he offered to sell the store to my dad.

And my dad was thrilled. Studio work was beginning to dry up for him as a new generation of musicians emerged, and he wanted out of the rat race anyway. A guitar store was the perfect fit for him.

"It's a really cool place," Lucas said. "People come from everywhere to buy guitars there."

I nodded. "One of the many reasons my parents decided to buy it."

"Do you play?" he asked.

I stifled a laugh, but not a grin, as I shook my head. "Uh, no. My dad's tried to teach me a few things, but I don't really have a gift for guitar the way he does."

He smiled at me. "Well, I know nothing about guitar, so you should show me what you've learned sometime."

I struggled not to crack up. As if I'd ever let him hear me fumble around with a guitar!

Mrs. Chadwick stood up to take attendance, just as the warning bell rang, and curbed our conversation.

CHAPTER FIVE

Over the course of the next couple of weeks, Luke and I settled in to a pattern of chatting before class. After our day off for Labor Day, he'd been in the parking lot after school each afternoon, and walked me to my car. The breezes became more and more blustery as summer pushed toward autumn, and the girly part of me found it terribly romantic to walk through the wind with Luke.

Of course, he was always on the way to cross-country practice, and I forced myself to acknowledge that his running was the only reason we ran into each other as I left school.

Despite my internal struggles to keep all things Lucas in the proper perspective, I discovered his reputation for being a nice guy was absolutely warranted. Whatever iffy feeling he'd had about me that first morning of school seemed to have disappeared. But I continued to be confused by his attention. He hadn't been anything more than friendly, but it all seemed very strange. High school boys weren't supposed to be friendly. They were either interested or uninterested, for a variety of reasons that usually had nothing whatsoever to do with the type of person you really were.

And besides, I was so ordinary, and Lucas was so... *not* ordinary.

Our quasi-friendship hadn't gone unnoticed. Jessie was constantly interested in what Luke and I talked about. I assured her over and over again it was nothing - that we talked only because we happened to be in lit class together. But she was certain more was going on and successfully swayed Marsha and Tiffany to her way of thinking.

Most of the time I just rolled my eyes at them when they suggested Lucas was interested in me as more than a friendly acquaintance.

But apparently, other kids had started to notice as well. Several times, when Lucas walked me to my car in the afternoon, his normal crowd of people – fellow runners Corey Jacobs and Will Harlow, I'd learned - just waved at him from across they way, rather than trying to get his attention or convince him to join them.

I'd never been the object of so much speculation in all my life. I felt uncomfortable with the attention I was attracting, but secretly thrilled during those moments when Luke chose me over his buddies. It was stupid, this crazy mix of feelings I had going on.

Even Kara, attempted to gain his attention without success, though her efforts were a little less conspicuous. The best I'd been able to figure out, without asking him outright, he and she were not getting back together.

Which made me happy. Which, in turn, pissed me off at myself.

And yes, I had to admit, I'd called Adrienne, several times, and given her the scoop on Lucas. I thought it couldn't hurt, since she was like ten states away. I missed her, but the "miss" was getting less and less the more I became a part of Sky Cove.

So, my first two weeks at Sky Cove Senior High were both easier and weirder than I imagined they would be.

It was my end-of-the-day locker stop that turned unfortunate, yet so very typical.

The piece of notebook paper taped to my locker read "Tennessee Hillbilly".

Fantastic. How long had that been there? I hadn't been to my locker since just after lunch, and nausea threatened as I thought about how many people could've seen the insult and had a laugh at my expense. It shouldn't matter. It shouldn't bother me. I *hated* that it did.

Looking around, the few kids in the hallway all seemed occupied with their own stuff. I grabbed the paper as nonchalantly as possible, and wadded it up.

Several lockers down, a girl named Phoebe, who had a very dark personality despite her sunny blond hair and seemed to like the "grunge" style of clothing, glanced over and said, "People in this school suck."

I figured she probably knew.

I tossed the wad of paper in the garbage on my way out of the building.

And so, the Friday of my second week ended, in many ways, the same as my first day. A few nice people, a lot of strangers, and a stupid teenage prank. Although, I did have to be a bit thankful it wasn't Miller-the-idiot and his vulgar joke this time.

Walking to my car, the afternoon sun was still warm, the heat of it a pleasant hum on my skin. And Lucas was there, taking my backpack and tossing it into the backseat.

I chose to forget about the hillbilly sign. Well, I chose to *try* and forget about it.

"So, you have big plans this weekend?" he asked.

"Not really." I fumbled around with my keys, taking longer than usual to unlock my door. Why was he asking about my weekend plans? "I work at the store on Saturdays until three, and after work Jessie and I are studying for our first chemistry test."

I opened my door, but instead of getting in, I turned back toward him.

"I remember Mr. Hartley's tests from last year," he said. "They can be lengthy."

"I was afraid of that," I laughed. "Fortunately, Jessie's good at it, so maybe she can help me get prepared. You have plans?"

"Cross-country meet this afternoon," he said. "First one of the season."

"Wow. Good luck, then."

"Thanks," Lucas nodded. He put his hands in his pockets and looked down at the ground, a kind of awkward gesture I hadn't seen from him before. "And listen, when you have the time, if you want a tour of the town, let me know. I'll be happy to show you around."

My brain broke in half, into two distinct and very different pieces. One part wanted desperately to believe Lucas was asking me out, because he liked me in *that* way. My heart hammered wildly, and my breath became shaky. The second part of my brain shouted loudly at the first part, declaring my stupidity at even considering such a ludicrous idea, furthermore ordering my heart to get itself under control.

In the end, I decided to believe the second part. It was much safer that way.

"Thanks," I replied, forcing my tone of voice to show absolutely no enthusiasm. At least I hoped so. "Maybe sometime."

He studied me for a second, and I wondered if I'd offended him. I mean, he'd seemed kind of nervous when he'd said it. As much as I didn't want my imagination running away with my heart in tow, I also didn't want to make him upset at me.

"I wanted to thank you again," I began. "Not just for rescuing me from Miller that first day, but also for being so nice to me. I didn't think I'd be able to make new friends this quickly."

"Well, you have." He smiled, pulling my driver's door open wider. "See you soon, Layla."

My name, spoken in his caramel smooth voice made my insides melt.

I cranked my car, but didn't pull out right away. Instead I pretended to dial my cell phone while I watched him walk away, black polo tucked into perfectly distressed blue jeans with a black, D-ring canvas belt at his waist.

And that first part of my brain went haywire all over again.

CHAPTER SIX

On my way to String City the following morning, I decided to take a scenic drive through town. Dad had gone in to open the store at nine o'clock, but he didn't expect me in until ten. Even now, the morning fog still lingered, gray and smoky, and atmospheric as all get out.

So, I took my time, winding my way through some of the old neighborhoods on my way to downtown Sky Cove.

The houses were beautiful, painted in both vibrant colors and bright whites. Many of them been carefully restored by owners who took great pride in their homes.

At the far end of Old Birch Lane a house stood alone, separated from the rest of the neighborhood. Swirled with fog, but still visible, I could tell it was older than the rest, both by the size and the look. It had a sort of character the other houses did not.

I couldn't help but slow down as I drove past. My foot moved to the brake almost of its own volition.

The house itself was nothing special. The black shutters stood in stark contrast to the chipping white paint. The main part of the house was an undersized rectangle, with a door in the center of the long wall and two windows on either side of the door. There was no porch or even a stoop with an overhang. An even smaller rectangle room – it couldn't have been any larger than a little bedroom – was attached to the main part of the house. One door and two tiny windows provided access to it.

From the road, I could make out two outbuildings behind the house. Both looked to be nothing more than shacks, and I wondered if the ramshackle look of them was natural or due in large part to painstaking restoration.

For a long moment, I stared at the house. It seemed beautiful to me, even though it was nothing compared to the other houses in the neighborhood. And, though I'd never seen it before, I felt a familiar connection to it I could not explain.

Inside me, strange emotions bumped into each other. It was as if I were stepping into a whirlpool of longing and joy and uncertainty and foreboding. Everything around me came into sharp focus. I was intensely aware of the cinnamon flavor of my chewing gum, the feel of the cool air coming from the vents, the sounds of the music coming from my car stereo. I felt my mind memorizing the moment for future reference.

I shook my head, trying to clear my thoughts. I accelerated slightly, pausing to appreciate the blueness of the sky and the cottony white clouds. Passing the driveway to the small little house that had captured my attention, I noticed it was an antique store. How appropriate, I thought, for the house that was obviously the oldest one in the neighborhood to be a showplace for treasures that had been seasoned with time.

I made a mental note to visit the Emerson House of Antiques as soon as possible. Like tomorrow.

For reasons I could not begin to fathom, I wanted to get inside that house.

***

My five-hour shift, which included a thirty-minute lunch break, had been productive. I'd swept the hardwood floors and dusted the counter and the shelves until the place smelled of homey, lemon furniture polish. I'd also helped Dad sell a beginner guitar to a young kid and his father, as well as a pricey Gibson Les Paul to a guitarist from down in Biddeford.

String City had a real vintage vibe, and not just from the classic guitars my dad had in stock. The dark hardwood on the floor and the light oak paneling on the walls gave the place an inviting appearance, and though Dad had a computer for ringing up purchases and printing receipts, he'd kept the old cash register on the counter, just for looks.

At three o'clock, I headed out the front door. My car was parallel parked a few spaces down from the storefront, and as I walked down the wide sidewalk, I looked around. It was pretty cool, to see the way people stopped and talked, or waved at each other from opposite sides of the street. People in Sky Cove knew one another.

Energy buzzed here, unlike anything I'd known before. Was it just the newness of life here that made me notice, or was there a magic in Sky Cove that didn't exist elsewhere?

On my way home, I couldn't resist driving back down Old Birch Lane, past the house that for some reason was the object of my intense curiosity. I wondered if my interest would be piqued or satisfied once I'd walked through the building. My questions would have to wait for another day, since I expected Jessie to arrive at my house any moment.

Right on time, she pulled into my driveway right after me, leaving her Mustang parked behind my Accord. She bounded out of the car, sunglasses pushed up on her head, and I realized that I was glad to see her. And not just because of her chemistry expertise.

She'd become a real friend, and the thought made me smile.

"Hey Jess!"

"Hi there." She pulled her backpack from the car and tossed the sunglasses to the front seat. "How was work?"

"Terribly exciting stuff," I said, heading up the front porch steps. "Sweeping and dusting."

"I think it's so cool that your dad's a musician," she said as I motioned for her to go in before me. "Was he ever in a band?"

"A couple of local ones." I shut the door behind me. "Mostly he did studio work, played for different artists on their recordings."

"That's so exciting!"

I'm sure dad's previous occupation sounded glamorous, but to me it was just the way things had always been.

"You know what else is exciting?" Jessie asked, wiggling her eyebrows like she always did when she had something interesting to share. "I heard we won the cross-country meet yesterday, and a certain handsome runner came in first."

"I have no idea who you're talking about." I rolled my eyes.

"Well, I know you're not crazy about chemistry, so I thought maybe a little Lucas news would make it more bearable."

Studying for the test turned out to not be so bad, and I actually felt prepared by the time Jessie left. We'd gone over our notes, re-read parts of the textbook, and, over a pepperoni pizza, had quizzed each other.

Afterward, I retreated to my room for some much-needed iPod time. The sun was fading fast, and though it was early for a Saturday night, I felt drained from work and chemistry overload.

I hit play, laid back, and closed my eyes.

The house I'd noticed this morning floated through that shadowy haze that happens when you close your eyes. It didn't take a lot of effort to imagine it newer, pristine, full of lively activity. I saw it change with the seasons, golden and red leaves falling in the yard, snow covering the roof, tiny green buds on the trees, and vibrant in the summer sun.

A woman opened the door, and I immediately knew she was happy. The scent of fresh bread escaped from the house, and anticipation coursed through her. She was waiting for something... or someone.

As if looking through the lens of a digital camera, I zoomed in on the woman standing in the door. I took note of her plain dress, the dingy white apron covering her bodice and skirt. She looked like she could've stepped right out of an episode of "Little House on the Prairie".

And then I saw her face. My breath caught in my chest, and my eyes widened in shock.

My own face stared back at me, with a smile so huge I wondered why her face didn't crack. She beamed with elation. I could feel her happiness in every molecule of my body.

Zooming my dream-lens back out, I saw the man walking through the yard toward her. He, too, looked like a throwback to the 1800s, with his boots and suspenders. Instantly, I knew he was coming home to her. To the woman who had my face.

I looked back to her. She smiled at him with such abandon. I felt the love that coursed through her for this man. This woman, who was me, but not me. She would sacrifice anything for him.

He was her life.

Panning back to the man, I looked to see if the joy I knew she felt was mirrored on his face.

It was. As I stared into his dark brown eyes, I knew he loved her every bit as much as she loved him.

It was plain and obvious, on Lucas Ellis's face.

CHAPTER SEVEN

Emerson House of Antiques was open on Sundays, unlike the downtown businesses like String City. So, after lunch and a quick read-through of my chemistry study notes, I headed out, on my way to Old Birch Lane.

It was an easy sell with my parents. I'd always loved used bookstores, consignment shops and the like, so it wasn't difficult for them to believe I was interested in antiques. And I was positive I would enjoy browsing through the store, even if seeing the inventory wasn't my first motivation.

Last night's dream ran through my mind again, as it had all day long. I'd never had a dream so vivid and alive. In the bright afternoon light, it was easy to tell myself that my mind had imprinted my face and Lucas's face on my dream-people simply because of the friendship we'd developed. Well, that *and* my over-active imagination where he was concerned.

But that was no explanation for the depth of *feeling* I'd experienced. I'd woken earlier than usual for a non-school day, and in the dim light of the morning, still warm under the covers of my bed, and before the sun broke over the horizon, I'd been swamped in the emotions of the dream. Love flooded through me, so strong it brought tears to my eyes. Feelings I had no experience with, or frame of reference for, burned bright inside my heart. And there in my bedroom, in the early morning hours, I'd cried softly for the beauty of the love between two people I did not know and who probably didn't exist.

It would've been humiliating had it not been in the privacy of my own room.

I wasn't sure what I thought a trip to Emerson's Antiques would solve, but it seemed the only thing to do after its appearance in my dream.

Two vehicles were parked in Emerson's circular driveway. A silver sedan was near the door, and behind it sat an older, dark green Ford Bronco. I decided the Bronco was probably a sensible choice, from what I'd heard about Maine winters.

I parked next to the Bronco and stepped out of my car. As usual, the air carried a salty, briny smell. It wasn't strong or unpleasant, but being so different from Tennessee, I always noticed it. I wondered if others here were aware of it, and figured they probably weren't. I liked to think that maybe Sky Cove was sharing a few of its secrets with me, to make me feel more at home.

As I headed to the front door, each step seemed filled with purpose, as if the short journey from my car to the store would somehow change everything.

Again, crazy, stupid thoughts.

It was unlike me to make a mountain out of a molehill, but over the past two weeks, I'd become quite proficient at it.

A bell jingled when I opened the front door, and I thought to myself that the place even smelled old. Not in an icky way, like an attic full of mold and dust, but rather like something cured to perfection by the passage of years.

To my left were cabinets filled with antique glassware. Fenton and Carnival glass, according to the labels, all of it sparkling and gleaming from the lights in the display cases. Directly in front of me were rows and rows of old stuff, dolls and dishes and books and costume jewelry. Beyond the front room, I could see another room, put together in much the same way... breakables and valuables in cases on the left side and other miscellaneous antiquated things on shelves in the middle section of the room.

I was just about to wander down the cabinets of pretty glassware when someone came in from the back room.

"Can I help you?" asked the attractive lady with dark auburn hair. I guessed her age at around thirty.

"Just looking around," I replied. "I noticed the place yesterday, and thought I'd come in and look around."

"You're new to Sky Cove?" She walked behind the counter, hopped up on a stool, and leaned across toward me, as if we were old friends having a conversation.

"I've been here about a month." I walked over and offered my hand. "I'm Layla Bradford. My dad's the new owner of String City."

"Oh, right," she said, shaking my hand. "I heard the place had changed hands. I'm Ashley Emerson."

I'd never put much stock in déjà vu, but if it could be described as a weird sense of impossible recognition, maybe this was it.

It really sort of wigged me out.

"I drove through this neighborhood on my way downtown yesterday, and I couldn't help but notice this house. It looks older than the rest." Wigged out or not, might as well see what I could learn about this place, and maybe figure out why it showed up in my dream last night.

"You're absolutely right," Ashley said. "It's been in my husband's family since the 1800's. Originally, it was the only house around and the rest of the area was used for crops or grazing animals."

My curiosity was definitely in overdrive, but I didn't want to make a pest of myself with questions about the house. After all, the dream had merely been a product of my subconscious anyway.

"Nice that it's still in your family," I said. "An antique store is a lovely way to showcase the house."

"It was my mother-in-law's idea," she answered. "She and I run the place together."

The ringing phone interrupted our conversation, so I began meandering through the store, stopping occasionally to look closer at some trinket that caught my attention. I tried to find some kind of feeling, some kind of vibe, but the more I focused on *trying* to feel something like what I'd felt in the dream, the more I felt nothing. I gave up and wandered into the back room.

And was hit full force with a wave of nostalgia. It was a physical feeling, chills on my skin and a pull in the pit of my stomach. A swell of yearning that took my breath, as if I'd walked into the most important place in all of history. But it was only little room full of old things, with one other customer besides me.

And that customer was wearing a brown tee shirt, tucked into a pair of nice jeans, with a brown leather belt at his waist, all of which accentuated the dark blond hair on his head.

And the dark brown eyes that turned and immediately locked on mine.

Lucas Ellis.

My brain shut down and simply refused to comprehend what it was seeing. Lucas was here, in this house, the very same one I'd dreamed about last night, the very same one he was coming home to, while I stood at the door and waited anxiously for him.

That *wasn't* me. And it *wasn't* him. It was a stupid, stupid dream. I reminded myself that I'd decided the dream was nothing more than a subliminal expression of my attraction to him.

But why was he here? No matter how I chose to compartmentalize the dream, Lucas being here today was one heck of a coincidence.

I don't know how long I stood there, no doubt looking like a complete loser, but at some point I realized he was talking to me.

And he was standing right in front of me.

"Layla?" he asked. "You okay?"

The sound of his voice snapped me out of it.

"Sorry." I blinked my eyes, shook my head. "Guess I was in a daze."

Good grief, could I be anymore of an idiot? Standing here, staring at him, acting catatonic in the middle of an antique store.

"Yeah, you kind of zoned out there for a minute."

Thanks so much for pointing that out.

"What are you doing here?" As soon as the words left my mouth, I knew they sounded snippy. I backpedaled quickly. "I mean, this is a rather weird place to run in to you."

"I could say the same," he said, smiling.

Man, his smile did things to me... the way it lit up his eyes. Made me feel all mushy and warm inside. And made me lose my train of thought.

What had he said? Oh yeah.

"I'm just killing some time," I said, scrambling to stay on topic. "I noticed this place on my way to the store yesterday, so I decided to come check it out."

"Yeah, I'm killing some time, too." He picked up a saltshaker that looked like a tiny bottle of Tequila. "What's the point in this?"

"Novelty, I suppose." I shrugged. "How often do you come here?"

Oh fantastic. That sounded like a corny come-on line. I could picture a poorly dressed man with too much cologne saying, in a smarmy voice, "Hey baby, do you come here often?"

If Lucas noticed, he didn't point it out or even grin. He just sat the margarita-esque saltshaker down and looked back up at me.

"Not a lot." He folded his arms across his chest, which pulled the brown tee shirt that matched the color of his eyes tight across his muscled upper body.

I ordered myself not to drool.

He continued. "I've been here a couple of times with my mom. She gets into weird stuff like this. I thought I might find something for her for Christmas."

"Wow, you're really on the ball. Christmas shopping right after Labor Day? And for your mother?"

"Well, like I said, my mom's into weird stuff. Sometimes it's hard to know what to get her."

I had a hard time believing that he'd come here, on a beautiful Sunday afternoon in September to buy a Christmas gift for his mother, but I decided to give him kudos for even thinking of it.

I made a mental note to add "appreciates his mother and treats her right" to my list of things to look for in the opposite sex.

Along with dark blond hair and chocolate brown eyes. And shirts that were always tucked in and looked neat.

I silently screamed at myself to get a grip. I changed the subject in an effort to get my thoughts under control.

"I heard you guys won the cross-country meet yesterday. Congratulations."

"Thanks," he said, moving to the next shelf of merchandise. "We ran well."

"I heard you ran exceptionally well. First place."

He shrugged. "It was a team effort."

Modesty. Another attribute to add to my list.

"Well, congratulations to you *and* the team."

Lucas just nodded. He picked up a clear glass paperweight, about the size of a baseball. Inside were white and silver moons and stars, some of which looked like they were shooting through the sky.

"This is an antique?" he asked.

I took it from him, turning it so I could read the bottom.

"1969," I said, handing it back to him. "Same year as the first moon landing."

"Ah, I get it." He held it up to the light. "My mom would like this. It's very mystical."

"Your mom sounds like an interesting lady."

"That's one way of putting it. But she's a great mom. You'd like her."

"Maybe I'll meet her sometime," I said.

I hoped that hadn't sounded pushy, or like I was trying to finagle more time with him. I'd meant only to continue the polite conversation we were having.

He looked at me, then glanced around the room as if making a decision, and finally looked back at the paperweight.

"Why don't come to my house with me? You can meet her." He held the paperweight up to my eye level. "You just have to promise not to tell her about the present I bought her."

As I looked at him through the swirling clear glass of the paperweight, his image shifted and turned. His face became thinner, his skin stubbly from several days growth of beard. His white shirt and brown suspenders dirtied and sweat-stained from a day's work outdoors.

Suspenders? White shirt?

This was not the Lucas I'd run into at the antique store. This was the Lucas from my dream.

I closed my eyes, forced them back open.

And saw him looking at me with a clean-shaven face.

The brown tee shirt had reappeared as well.

"How about it? Want to come over?"

"Um, I don't know." I blinked several times, trying to clear my thoughts. "I guess it would be okay. I'd have to run it past my parents first."

"No problem," he said. "I'll pay for this, then follow you back to your house. You can introduce me to your folks, so they know you're not headed off with a total stranger, then I'll drive you to my house and back."

Well, I guess he had it all figured out. This sounded strangely like the offer of a tour of Sky Cove he'd made in the school parking lot on Friday afternoon. Again, I didn't know exactly how to take it.

Was there more to it than a friendly visit? Were his intentions platonic or...

Stop it! Stop it!

I could not afford to have delusions of grandeur about Lucas. I reminded myself once again that girls like me did not attract the attention of boys like him. At least not in a romantic way.

Friends. We were friends. And there was nothing wrong with two friends hanging out together on a Sunday afternoon.

"Okay," I said, following him to the cash register. "I'd like to meet your mom."

CHAPTER EIGHT

Lucas charmed my parents as completely as he charmed me. He followed me to my house and met my parents, and afterward he probably could've gotten them to hand over their bank account number and credit card information.

Mom looked at me with a smile and a gleam in her eyes as Lucas and I walked out the front door. I knew she thought there was more to Luke's visit. I'd have to set her straight when I got home.

In the passenger side of his Bronco I ran through that conversation in my mind, planning what I'd say to Mom to convince her that he and I were not a romantic item.

"You look like you're in deep thought," he said, expertly shifting the gears on his manual transmission. I'd never seen a boy drive a stick shift before. There was something really hot about a guy with one hand on the steering wheel and one hand on the gearshift, driving like it was the easiest thing in the world.

"Just thinking about something I need to tell my mom," I answered.

Just past Sky Cove Harbor, he turned off the main highway that bisected the town and onto White Bridge Road.

Trees lined the narrow road like canopies, creating shadows on the pavement that looked liked an artist's brushstrokes.

"Your parents are really nice," he said. "I'll have to come by the guitar store sometime and look around."

"You mentioned your mom. Is your dad around?"

Lucas shook his head. "No, he's been gone a long time. I don't think he was much into being a family man."

Immediately I wished I hadn't asked. "I'm sorry. I shouldn't have asked you that. It was rude."

"It's okay," he assured me. "It's not a sore spot or anything, so don't worry."

We turned a corner, and crossed a bridge that was indeed white, and a house came into view. It was a small, yellow, two-story cottage, complete with gingerbread in the corners of the front porch. In the front yard was a little garden. It looked to be thriving, though I had no idea what was growing there. A green thumb I was not.

Somehow, I did not feel surprise when Lucas turned into the driveway of the yellow cottage. I could tell by looking that whoever lived here knew what it meant to take care of people and things, and it was obvious by his personality someone had cared a great deal about him.

He pulled in and set the parking brake, sliding the bag with the paperweight out of sight under his seat. I opened my door and hopped out, just as he came around to my side of the Bronco.

"I was going to get your door for you." He folded his arms across his chest and looked at me with a smile.

"Really?" Did guys still do that these days? I'd only ever seen it on old movies.

"Really," he said. "Like I told you before, my mom's real big on treating girls with respect."

I silently wondered if Lucas had any faults. I was starting to think he didn't.

"Come on. Let's go in." He reached over and took my hand.

Everything inside me went on alert when he touched me. He didn't hold my hand with force, but rather with a gentle firmness that was comforting and secure.

My heart swelled, almost to the point of pain. It was the sweetest feeling I'd ever experienced. And it scared me to death. The perfection of my hand in his overwhelmed me, and I had to stop myself from clutching his fingers in response to the feelings churning inside me.

We took the steps up to the porch side-by-side, hands still entwined. When we reached the door, he let go of my hand and opened it, gesturing for me to go in first.

It appeared chivalry was not dead.

"Hey Mom!" he called, as we stepped inside the house, and the scent of chocolate wafted toward me.

I assumed this room was the living room, because there was a cushy looking sofa, a recliner, and a flat screen television mounted on the wall. But those were the only things that defined this room as the living area. The rest of the room looked like a cross between a library and a museum.

Two walls were lined with floor-to-ceiling bookshelves, crammed full of books of every size and color. In front of the books sat knick-knacks of all sorts – vases, blown glass animals, wooden carvings that looked Native American, even sets of pewter cups and pitchers. A third wall was covered with postcards, almost to the point of being wallpapered with them. From where I stood, I couldn't tell where many of them were from, but I did see the Eiffel Tower and a large waterfall of some sort on a couple of them.

I could see no apparent theme or organization, but it was oddly soothing, and I liked the sense of randomness.

"My mom collects stuff," Lucas whispered, leaning his face close to my ear. He took my hand again, just as his mother came in the room.

My heart lurched into my throat.

"Lucas! This must be Layla!" She breezed in to the room, almost ethereally. And she was beautiful. Younger than I'd imagined, with blond hair that fell in soft waves almost to her waist. She wore brown cargo pants and a bright blue tee shirt, and leather flip-flops. If I didn't know better, I'd have thought her a college student.

"I've sort of told her about you," he said, his fingers squeezing mine.

He really had to stop touching me if he wanted me to be coherent.

Yeah, right. Like I wanted that to happen.

"Mom, this is Layla Bradford."

"And I'm Gwen Ellis." To my surprise, she pulled me in to a quick, but fierce hug. "You can call me Gwen."

When she let me go, the smile on her face was beaming. I noticed her eyes were the same deep brown of Luke's.

His hand found mine again, softly enclosing my fingers with his own. My head swam. I wondered if my eyes were rolling back into my head.

"And your dad owns String City, I hear," Gwen was saying, motioning us to follow her out of the living room.

"Yes ma'am."

"Oh don't call me ma'am," she said over her shoulder. "It'll make me feel old."

We walked through the living room, across a hallway, and into the kitchen. It was small, but cozy, with yellow walls, and blue and white checked tile on the countertops.

"I finished the brownies," she said to Luke. "You two have a seat."

We sat, as instructed, while Gwen uncovered a plate full of the source of the chocolate smell that had greeted us at the front door.

"So, String City is your family's business." She pulled bright blue bowls from a cabinet, and I watched with wide-eyes as she placed a huge brownie in each one.

"That's right," I answered.

"Her parents are Jack and Michelle Bradford, Mom," Lucas put in.

Gwen walked to the refrigerator. She opened the freezer and took out a gallon of ice cream. The she reached into the fridge and came out with chocolate syrup and maraschino cherries.

Holy cow. Luke's mom was making brownie sundaes.

The three of us sat at the table in the eat-in kitchen, each with a huge dessert. The warm brownie, cold creamy ice cream, and syrupy chocolate were enough to overdose my taste buds, in a good way.

Gwen was easy to talk to. She listened intently and laughed easily, her lyrical voice drawing me in like a beautiful song. I liked her a great deal.

It was more than obvious how Lucas had turned out the way he had. With a mother like that, there was no way he could've been a jerk.

She even excused herself after the brownies were eaten, giving Luke and me a few moments alone. We sat in the living room, and he explained that he and his mom hadn't traveled much, but she knew people who did and she had them send her postcards from wherever they went.

Gwen had made the necessary sacrifices to raise a son on her own, which meant no expensive vacations. He said one day he wanted to take her to Alaska to see the Northern Lights. It was where she most wanted to go.

Nope, Lucas had no faults.

Before we left, we slipped down the hall and found his mom in her office, typing away on the medical transcription that she did from home. She stood up when she saw us at the door.

"Oh Layla, I'm so glad you came to visit." She hugged me again, and, not so startled by it this time, I hugged her back. Eagerly. She lowered her voice to a whisper at my ear. "My Lucas hasn't smiled this much in a long time."

Apparently she had the wrong idea about us, too.

But as Lucas took my hand and walked me back through the house, I had to admit that I could see why she did. It was becoming difficult for me to keep things in perspective myself.

When we got to the Bronco, he opened the door for me, and I was bowled over again by what a gentleman he was.

Gwen stood at the door, smiling in approval as Lucas came around the front to slide in the driver's seat. He looked back at his mother and nodded back.

Something strange passed between them, something other than the close mother-son bond they clearly shared. It almost seemed like some silent form of communication, some kind of private exchange that only they understood. Gwen smiled once more and disappeared into the house.

And, odd as it was, I discovered Luke's wordless discussion with his mother only endeared him to me more.

I was *so* in trouble.

CHAPTER NINE

The next two weeks passed in a sort of blur, cooler temperatures, blustery winds, socializing, and homework. The routine I'd grown accustomed to continued, with one exception.

Lucas now walked with me after literature, and delivered me to the door of my third period class. He didn't hold my hand at school, but that didn't matter. The thrill still barreled through me every day as we meandered through the crowded hallways together.

People looked at us, curious. It seemed I was doomed to be the center of attention at Sky Cove Senior High, though I didn't seem to be so annoyed by it anymore. I was becoming a bit more comfortable in the spotlight. Not that I would ever love it, but if I was there because Lucas was by my side, I couldn't complain.

I still struggled to maintain a distance, at least emotionally, from Lucas, which was proving more and more difficult all the time. I knew at some point it would become futile, but my sense of self-preservation demanded that I not allow my heart to become entangled all the way.

Each time I reminded myself that Lucas and I were just friends, a little voice inside me responded with, "Yeah, right."

He'd still made no move that would indicate he wanted things to go further between us. But it appeared the attention he paid to me caused other boys to take notice.

Which was attention I neither needed nor wanted.

Since Monday of this week, I'd been asked out for the weekend twice, each time politely declining. It had been somewhat awkward, since the invitations had come from Robbie Taylor and Chris Andersen, who were part of the crowd that Jessie, Marsha, Tiffany, and I sat with at lunch. I was friendly with both of them, and I didn't want my non-interest in dating them to undermine that.

Wednesday I'd noticed Zack Weston hanging around my locker after first period, looking as if he wanted to talk to me. Thankfully, my daily visit with the girls gave him no opportunity to get a word in, and he pretty much just stood there the whole time, staring at the dirty once-white-but-now-gray tiles on the floor. He didn't try to talk to me after literature, because by Wednesday it seemed everyone knew Lucas walked me to my third period class.

It was Thursday now. Jessie waited for me in the parking lot, and as we walked into school together, I hoped the barrage of interest from other guys was over.

If I were really honest with myself, I would admit there was only one boy I wanted.

I scanned the front lobby for Luke's six-foot two-inch frame, coming up empty. Sometimes he was there, but most of the time he put in a few miles of running before school.

The boy who'd given me the head-nod on the first day of school stood at the edge of the lobby, with Luke's ex, Kara Jennings, and a few other kids whose names I didn't know yet. I'd since learned the head-nodder's name was Lance Garrett.

He approached Jessie and me, falling into step with us as we made our way down the hall. The warning bell had yet to ring, so the hallway was easy to navigate. Most kids were still hanging around in the lobby.

"So Layla," Lance said. "How's it going? You adjusting to Sky Cove okay?"

"I am, thanks."

Jessie elbowed me from my other side. She could see what was coming.

"Well, I was wondering," he began. "There's a home football game tomorrow night, and I thought maybe you'd like to go with me. We could go hang out at The Pizza Place afterward. Everybody gets together there, so it would be like a group date."

Lance was supremely confident, and I wondered where that had come from. It had been my experience that many times shorter-than-average boys were insecure. I wondered if my rejection would damage his self-image, or if he'd laugh it off and decide I had no idea what I was missing out on.

"Thanks for the invitation, Lance," I began. Over the past couple of days I'd perfected my thanks-but-no-thanks routine. "I appreciate you thinking of me, but I'm really not ready to start dating yet."

Lance looked at me sideways, tilting his head as if considering my words.

I went on. "I may be at the game, and maybe even at The Pizza Place after, but I'm still just getting to know everyone."

He nodded, that same too-cool nod he'd given me the first day. Apparently he was going with the "she doesn't know what she's missing" response to rejection.

"Probably not a bad idea," he said. "Maybe I'll see you there."

"Sure," I said, just as we reached the door to the chemistry room, where Jessie and I had our first class.

"See you around, Layla."

And Lance was gone.

He'd handled it pretty well, with no hint of awkwardness. Of course, he was a senior and not a part of the crew I socialized with.

The warning bell rang, creating a sea of people in the hallway. Jessie and I stood just outside the chemistry room, about to step in, when Kara Jennings breezed past us, bumping me slightly in the shoulder.

She was never in this hallway, at least not at this time of day. Still standing near the door, I saw her look at me, a slight smile on her face. It didn't reach her eyes, and I wondered if her trip down this hall had been to spy on my response to Lance's invitation.

I wanted to feel smug... to think about the fact that Luke wasn't with her anymore and for whatever reason had developed a friendship with me. The thought that Kara Jennings, tall and glamorous in every sense of the word, might be jealous of me should've brought smile to my face.

Instead, I just felt small and insignificant.

However, it was worth a tiny grin to think that she was not really so confident when it came to Lucas.

Jessie saw my smile, and we shared a little chuckle before sinking down in our seats.

***

During literature, Lucas said nothing about the home football game. Of course I knew he had a cross-country meet immediately after school on Friday, which would run him right up until game time.

And really, what had I expected? We were, after all, just friends.

He still walked me to my third period U.S. History class, though, and our presence still garnered looks from other students.

At the door to Mr. Boyd's classroom, he stopped me.

"Are you coming to the game tomorrow?" He leaned a shoulder against the door facing, angling his head so our eyes met.

My heart raced like a thoroughbred at the Kentucky Derby. The struggle to keep massive eagerness from my voice was huge.

"Jessie and I were talking about going," I answered, forcing myself to talk slow and even. "And maybe meeting up with Marsha and Tiffany."

"I have to run tomorrow afternoon, but it's a home meet, so I don't have to travel." He reached for my backpack, taking it off my shoulder. He did it so absently that I knew he didn't even think about it. The lightness of my shoulders mirrored the buoyancy I felt in my heart. "I'll have to go home and take a shower after I run, but I should be there by half-time."

Exactly what was he saying?

The question must've shown on my face, because he quickly added, "I'd like to sit with you, if you don't mind."

How in the world could I mind that? Had he never looked in a mirror?

"Of course I don't mind," I answered, a giant smile spreading across my face.

Though I was still unsure. Had he asked me to be his date? He'd only mentioned sitting with me.

"You look surprised," he said.

"Well, I... um," I stammered. I took a deep breath and went on. "I just figured you had your own crowd of people you hung out with at ball games."

He just shrugged. "I don't really have a usual crowd of people, unless you count the cross-country team."

"Oh." I could think of nothing else to say.

"I heard you'd had a few invitations to the game already," he said. "And that you'd turned them all down."

"Small school gossip." I rolled my eyes. "No secrets around here, huh?"

"Not so much," he laughed.

I had to be careful here. I couldn't give him the same story about not being ready to start dating, because when it came to him, that wasn't really true. But I also couldn't tell him that the real reason I'd turned Robbie, Chris, and Lance down was because I only wanted to date *him*.

This entire situation was ludicrous. What had I gotten myself into?

"If I turned anyone down, it wasn't because I wasn't flattered," I said. "It was because it just didn't feel right."

"Well, if it doesn't feel right sitting with me, just say so," he said, smiling.

"That won't be necessary." I smiled back, reaching for my backpack.

He pulled my backpack out of reach, put a hand on the small of my back, and guided me into the room.

I was amazed that I could walk on legs that now felt like jelly.

My seat was in the second row, and Lucas dropped my bag right next to it. All around us, people stared.

"If I don't see you after school, I'll see you tomorrow in lit class." He smiled again, turning to head for the door and to his own third period.

"Thanks Luke." I gestured to the backpack on the floor.

"No problem."

CHAPTER TEN

Friday the school buzzed with activity and excitement about the football game. In the hallways, it was all anyone talked about. The girls talked about what they were wearing, and guys talked about washing their cars and their plans for after the game.

Small town, small school must equal first home football game being the event of the school year.

Despite my better judgment, I told Jessie about my conversation with Lucas about the game. She was sure it meant something. I was still shoving my enthusiasm into a black hole full force.

During our walk from literature to U.S. History, Lucas reiterated that he'd be at the game by half time, and he'd find me when he got there.

I walked around the rest of the day in a sort of haze, waffling between exhilaration and dread. It was confounding, not being able to decide how to feel.

At lunch Jessie asked me what I was wearing, and I actually gave in and discussed wardrobe matters with her. Heaven help me, I'd succumbed to girl talk.

But, it turned out to be worth it because by the time I left school that afternoon, I had a plan. Distressed blue jeans, a baby pink tee shirt, and a navy blue sweater that I could button up if necessary. Because, this was Maine after all, and September nights got chilly. I also settled on my brown leather slip on boots. They weren't cowgirl boots or anything, but I decided it would be a nice testament to my southern heritage, since they did look like they were ready for mucking stalls or driving a tractor.

Neither of which I'd ever done.

Walking through the parking lot toward my car, with the sky overcast and the breeze just this side of cool, I realized that somewhere between lunch and now, I'd decided to be excited after all.

Then I saw Miller-the-idiot standing next to my Honda.

Great. My mood was now sour.

"Layla," he said. "I wanted to apologize."

I should be forgiving, I knew. But he'd embarrassed me so much that forgiveness was hard to find.

However, it had kicked off whatever it was that was going on between Lucas and me, so I supposed I should be, if not grateful, at least somewhat accepting.

"Okay." I stopped at the front of my car, not willing to walk in the narrow space between it and the SUV parked beside me. It would put me much too close to Miller.

"I was a stupid jerk," Miller went on. "I'm surprised Luke didn't punch me. But that wouldn't be like him."

"Yes, you were a jerk," I replied, my attitude softening at the mention of Lucas. "But I guess we all can be sometimes, so I'll accept your apology."

"Good," he nodded, backing out of the space between the vehicles. "I'll see you later."

He took off in the direction of the football field, gym back slung across his back.

Well, would wonders never cease?

***

At home, I was so keyed up I could barely sit still. I ironed my clothes and laid them out and freshened up my make up, but that only managed to kill about an hour. I wasn't expecting Jessie to pick me up for another two hours. I decided I could use some mellowing out, so I grabbed my iPod and curled up on my bed.

I really wanted to be smooth and cool about the whole situation. I hated that I was tied in knots.

I only meant to relax, to get my mind off the intense anticipation I felt about seeing Lucas at the game. But the subtle jazz sounds drifting through my consciousness soon had me dozing.

At first, I knew I was dreaming. The pictures in my mind were all of lovely places in Sky Cove, and I saw them all as if I was flying above the town, just high enough to see everything, but not so high that I couldn't see the details.

When my flight took me over Old Birch Lane, the autopilot that was choosing my direction stopped and hovered over Emerson's Antiques. At first, I saw the silver sedan, and knew Ashley was inside working.

My lips curved into a smile when I remembered seeing Lucas there. As if taking instructions from my thoughts, I felt myself being lowered to the ground behind the house, directly outside the window to the back room.

I watched from outside as Lucas and I talked about the paperweight he chose for his mother. It was the strangest feeling, standing outside the house, yet seeing myself inside. Dreams really could play tricks on you, couldn't they?

As the thought entered my mind, the image in front of me changed. Suddenly I no longer saw Lucas and myself as we were that day in the antique store. Instead, I saw the versions of us from my previous dream.

The room wasn't filled with shelves of antiques, but was instead almost barren. A miniature wooden table sat off to one side of the room, with two plain chairs. What looked to be a wood stove was on the opposite end.

We were worried about something, Lucas and me. I couldn't hear our voices, but I could see the concern on our faces. Tears streamed down my face as Lucas did his best to console me.

I knew something was terribly wrong. In my heart I knew Lucas was trying to leave. Not because he didn't love me, but because he believed it was necessary to keep me safe. I wanted to beg him to stay, but deep inside I knew that to stay would mean his death.

I watched as Lucas put his arms around me and held me. Even from my place on the grass outside, I could feel the warmth and the strength of his embrace. I cried harder as he whispered something in my ear, clinging to him with all my might. How I wished I could understand what he was saying.

My heart splintered in two as he turned and walked toward the back door, the love that was inside spilling over into my being until it bubbled over. The injustice of what was happening washed over me in violent waves that brought me to my knees.

Through the window, I read Lucas's lips as he said one last "I love you" then walked out the door.

The finality of the door closing behind him echoed like thunder in my mind.

CHAPTER ELEVEN

"Layla!"

My eyes flew open and I looked around frantically, assuring myself that I was in my bedroom. Mom stood in my doorway.

"Jessie's here," she said.

I yanked the headphones out of my ears and...

Two hours? I'd only meant to unwind. How had I managed to sleep for two hours?

And the dream... it had been so real, so vivid. I was trembling, and even now I wanted to sob in despair.

"I fell asleep," I answered, as if she hadn't already figured that out. "Tell Jessie I'll be right down."

At least my clothes were ready, which was more than I could say for my hair. I dressed in a matter of seconds and pushed my feet into my boots, pulling the bottoms of my boot-cut jeans over the tops. Running across the hall to the bathroom, I twisted my hair into a messy knot and secured it into place with a large clip. It wasn't my first choice for a hair-do, but it looked good enough, sort of casually elegant.

I pulled a few wavy strands loose to hang around my face, then brushed a bit of pink blush across my cheeks. I grabbed my eyeliner pencil and spruced up a bit around my eyes. Apparently, I'd cried during the dream, because the liner I'd applied before my impromptu nap was all but invisible.

Satisfied that I looked acceptable, I ran down the stairs to find Jessie. She was waiting in the kitchen, having a lively conversation with my mother about our cross-country team.

I groaned to myself. I'd only barely managed to convince Mom that Lucas was just my friend. If Jessie brought up that Lucas was meeting me at the game Mom would be all over me again.

"Hey Jess," I said, picking my purse up off the table. "Ready?"

"Sure." Jessie was all smiles, and thankfully she ceased her talk about the cross-country runners before Luke's name was mentioned.

The football stadium was packed, the stands overflowing with people, most of them kids from Sky Cove. Our opponents, from nearby Camden, made up a smaller portion of the crowd.

Jessie and I found seats near the top of the stands on the Sky Cove side. Marsha and Tiffany found us soon after. With the sun now below the horizon, the air felt chilly and crisp, but not at all unpleasant. Perfect football weather. Of course, I knew next to nothing about football, other than what a touchdown was. But I quickly figured out that, for most of the students here, the game was more of a social occasion than a sporting event.

I had to make myself refrain from looking around for Lucas. It would be too obvious, to my friends and probably to everyone else.

But it was so hard not to. Not only because I looked forward to being with him, but because the feelings from my dream were still hanging around, nagging at my heart. In the dream, I had been devastated by Lucas's departure. Heartbroken by his tearful "I love you" as he left.

And though I knew it had only been a dream, it was proving difficult to convince my emotions that the real, live Lucas was fine and exactly as he had been at school today. That he hadn't decided to skip town for my well being the way dream-Lucas had.

Or that he hadn't decided being friends with the new girl was too much of a liability.

And didn't it just make me so happy to have those doubts bouncing around my head?

Three minutes remained in the second quarter when I felt a hand on my shoulder.

"Room for me?" asked Lucas. The noise from the crowd was loud, so his face was bent to my ear. His voice, deep, rich and full of amusement, made my heart melt.

Relief flooded through me as I scooted closer to Jessie, making room for Lucas on the end of the bleacher. I knew the smile on my face was gigantic, both from Luke's presence beside me and the release of tension that had tormented me since the dream.

"Did you win?" I asked, leaning closer to make myself heard.

"Yes." He smiled. "We did."

"Did *you* win?"

He nodded, but like last time, he clearly didn't think much of his own success.

I was very aware of Jessie, Marsha, and Tiffany - and probably a lot of other people - watching us. I didn't want to say or do anything that would make him uncomfortable or give anyone the wrong idea about us.

Despite the way I felt about him, I still had no idea exactly *what* we were. And though it was sometimes frustrating to be so uncertain, I was really enjoying getting to know him without any expectations or pressure.

He slipped on a gray hooded sweatshirt, bearing the Sky Cove cross-country logo, then picked up my hand.

"Glad to see you, Layla." He winked, then playfully kissed the back of my hand.

69

He laid my hand on my knee, then positioned his own knee so that the side of his hand brushed against mine. Perfect and sweet, the subtle gesture proved Lucas to be a romantic. And, unlike the ending of my dream, <u>here</u>.

I swallowed past the lump of joy in my throat.

CHAPTER TWELVE

As far as successes went, the last Friday of September had been a big one for Sky Cove Senior High. Lucas and the cross-country team won their meet, and the football team won soundly over their rival. Apparently, Todd Miller had even been the MVP of the game.

The football stands began to empty, and all over the stadium, kids started making plans to continue the evening somewhere else. The Pizza Place was the most popular choice, I gathered from what Jessie and the girls said, because it had picnic seating outside to accommodate larger crowds.

And though the breeze was chilly, it wasn't uncomfortable outside, even this late in the evening.

"You guys ready?" Jessie asked, looking to Luke and me. Over her shoulder Marsha and Tiffany looked on.

"Sure," I said, looking up at Lucas. I had no idea if he was planning to go with us.

"Did you drive?" he asked me.

I shook my head. "I rode with Jessie."

"You want to ride with me?"

The girls giggled, in that way only girls can do.

Marsha shouted, "Of course she does!" and Jessie and Tiffany immediately agreed. Jessie promised to save us a seat at their table, and also to bring my purse, which was still in her car.

Luke and I didn't hurry as we walked to his Bronco. Having arrived at the game late, he'd had to park a good distance away, in the parking lot of the elementary school on the other side.

He took my hand again and led me through the crowd of people in the direction of his car. When we'd left most of the noise behind us, he leaned closer to me.

"I thought about you this afternoon." His voice was soft, almost unsure, as if testing my reaction.

"While you were running?

"Yes. Sometimes I - " he broke off. "Sometimes I let my mind wander while I run."

"And you thought about me?" I was rather stunned by his admission.

"I wondered what you were doing, how you were feeling, what you'd look like tonight." One corner of his mouth lifted in a smile.

Breath became difficult to draw. Was there another guy on the planet who was this good with words?

"So," he went on. "How did you feel this afternoon?"

"If you mean was I excited about the game tonight," because no way could I get into the dream business, "I was."

"That's good." He squeezed my hand. "So was I."

When we reached the Bronco he proved himself a gentleman once more and opened my door. He cranked the ignition, and in minutes we arrived at The Pizza Place.

We drew looks from the gang when we walked in, although the looks no longer lingered into stares. I supposed seeing us together had become common.

Music blared from overhead speakers while kids laughed and chattered. The scents of tomato and garlic filled the room as surely as the exuberance of the crowd.

Jessie and the girls had secured a table inside, and Lucas and I joined them there. Soon after, Corey and Will, Luke's cross-country teammates took a seat at our table. The voices inside the restaurant were almost as loud as they were at the game, a constant stream of talking and laughing that you could almost feel.

Words began to form in my mind again, forcing the buzz from all the talking to the background. They flitted through my consciousness, seeming random and meaningless at first. The feeling was as disconcerting as it had been at school that first day, and though I tried to focus on what I was seeing, I found it impossible to pinpoint the origin of the thoughts. It was as if they weren't mine, as if I were somehow picking up on the thoughts of another person in the room.

The idea was so implausible I almost laughed at myself, but that didn't stop me from looking around the room. Aside from the people at our table, I saw various faces I recognized from school even though I didn't know their names. Others I remembered, such as Lance the head-nodder and Miller the idiot.

I closed my eyes, and once again the sentence formed behind my lids.

It won't be long now, my love.

The words might've sounded mysteriously romantic under other circumstances, but as it was all they did was creep me out. The vibe it gave me felt almost threatening.

Luke touched my arm, and I opened my eyes. The haze lifted from my mind, and I rejoined my friends, deciding the anti-social moment was nothing more than over-excitement.

The conversation bounced from school romances to who got caught cheating in Calculus and everything in between. I discovered that Lucas seemed just as comfortable in a large group as he was one-on-one. There was no hand holding at the table, but he was attentive and polite, getting up to refill my drink twice and discreetly refusing to let me chip in my share on the pizza.

It was then I realized that this had turned into a date.

Some girls might have been disappointed that he wasn't more obvious about it, but for me, the fact that he kept things just between us made them all the more special.

I had no choice but to admit to myself that our friendship was moving in the romantic direction. And all the caution and self-preservation in the world could not keep me from being ecstatic about it.

"Drive you home?" he asked in a soft whisper at my ear, as things began to wind down. "Or would you rather ride with Jessie?"

My heart swelled to the point that I thought my chest would no longer be able to contain it. I had never known a more perfect night.

"I'll go with you."

"Will it be okay with your parents if I drive you home?"

"Yes. My mom thinks you hung the moon."

"That's good," he said. "Though it's not your mom I'm most interested in impressing."

We said our goodbyes, and no one seemed surprised when we left together, though Robbie and Lance eyed us a bit more than everyone else. I couldn't find it in me to feel guilty. After all, I hadn't exactly lied to them. And it wasn't as if I'd turned them down and then accepted an invitation from Lucas.

I realized then why he'd been so careful to *not* ask me to be his date. It was so the things I'd told the other boys when I turned them down would still be true.

He insisted on walking me to the door when we arrived at my house, and exchanged polite hellos with my mother, who had waited up, and was, of course, thrilled to see him.

She excused herself – my mom was cool like that – and headed off to bed.

Luke stayed where he was beside the front door.

The quiet of my house after the noise at the game and the pizza place was a welcome invasion. I took off my sweater, hanging it across the back of a chair, enjoying the way the cool September air felt against my skin.

"I'd hang out with you a little longer," he said, "but I don't know that I could stay awake."

"You haven't stopped all day," I said. "School, your meet, the game."

"It's been a good day. A better night." He picked up my hand, held it in both of his. "Can we do this again sometime? Maybe just the two of us?"

I laughed. I was helpless to stop it. This whole night had been amazing and ridiculous and astonishing, and my mind just couldn't keep up.

Lucas was interested in *me*. In *that* way.

"Is this where you tell me you're not ready to start dating?" he asked with a smirk. "That you're still getting to know everyone?"

"You heard that?" I asked, my giggling finally dying down a bit.

"Told you before, news travels fast." He grinned, crossed his arms over his chest, and leaned against the door, waiting for an answer.

"I was honest when I said those things," I said. "When I said them to Robbie and Chris and Lance."

"Lance asked too?" He seemed surprised.

I nodded. "Yesterday."

"And you told him the same thing?"

"Yes. And it was true when I said it to him." I leaned against the doorframe, putting myself a bit closer to him. "But it wouldn't be true if I said it to you right now."

"Is that a yes?" He reached out and tucked a wisp of hair behind my ear. "Will you go out with me? On a proper date?"

My skin tingled where his fingers brushed against my cheek. All the breath in my lungs backed up and I had to remind myself to breath.

"I'm not sure how it could be more proper than tonight," I whispered when I found my voice again. "But, yes. I'd love to go out with you."

"A proper date means just us," he smiled. "And something a bit more grand than a loud ballgame and a crowded pizza parlor."

"Okay." I refused to let my mind start imagining what he might have in store.

He pulled his cell phone from his pocket and held it up. "Can I have your number? So I can call you?"

I tried to remember the last time someone *asked* for my number. These days, with cell phones more common in school than pencils, most people just traded phones and put their own numbers in.

I reached in my purse and retrieved my own. "Only if I can have yours, too."

When we'd exchanged numbers and stored them in our cells, he picked up my hand again and stepped closer.

My heart hammered, my pulse thundering in my ears. I hadn't given much thought to sharing a first kiss with Lucas, but darned if I wasn't excited about it now.

"We'll talk soon, Layla," he said, looking me directly in the eyes. "Thank you for tonight."

"I should be thanking you. For the pizza and for driving me around."

He shook his head. "My pleasure."

And then he lowered his head. I watched his face move closer to mine, braced for something I knew would be spectacular.

To my surprise, he pressed a soft, warm kiss to my forehead. His lips lingered, for several seconds, and I closed my eyes, letting the beauty of the moment spread through me. He didn't smell like fancy cologne, but rather soap and laundry detergent, a combination that on him was pleasant and welcoming.

His gentle kiss was more intimate and meaningful than any lip-lock driven by passion could have been.

He didn't say goodbye as he left. He just smiled, walking backwards down the porch steps and sidewalk, all the way to his truck.

And I stood in the door, grinning like a fool.

***

Lucas floated through my dreams again, and for once I wasn't surprised. A few times I roused awake, just enough to realize I was dreaming and remember the evening we'd just spent together.

I was quite sure the smile was present on my face even as I slept.

Images of us from the game morphed into new images. The two of us walking along the beach, the cool fall air whipping around us. Running along the water's edge, cold salt water splashing our bare feet and dampening the bottoms of our jeans.

Suddenly I was running alone, my dress soaked with the cold rain falling from the sky. An urgency clawed at me, and I pushed my legs to run faster. Fear coursed through me as I called for him, though the screams that left my throat were silent.

I had to run harder. If I wasn't fast enough all would be lost. I would not be able to save him.

An outcropping of rocks came into sight, jutting out from a hillside that almost reached the water. Though my dream was soundless, in my mind I could hear voices on the other side of the rocks. Angry voices. Violent voices.

I opened my mouth to scream at them to stop, the noiseless action ripping from my body. The men with angry voices could not hear me over their own shouting.

I neared the rocks, terrified of what I might find on the other side.

My mind heard the pounding sounds, a beating thud that happened over and over again. And I knew.

They were hurting him.

I dropped to the wet sand and shrieked.

I wasn't silent anymore.

CHAPTER THIRTEEN

The shaking woke me up. At first I thought it was because of the cold rain and the grief in my heart. It took me a few seconds to realize it was my mom.

"Layla, wake up!"

My eyes finally unglued. Mom sat on my bed, arms on my shoulders, and when she saw my eyes open, she gently framed my face between her hands.

"Since when do you have nightmares?" she whispered. "What in the world were you dreaming about?"

I blinked my eyelids in an effort to clear the fog from my brain. "I can't remember." It was a lie, and I felt bad about it even as the scratchy words left my mouth. But I couldn't tell her the truth. It would sound ridiculous. Not only that, but the pain that was still slicing through my heart would make it impossible to contain my anguish if I tried to talk about it out loud.

"What time is it?" I hoped I hadn't woken my parents.

"It's almost nine," she answered. "Your dad's almost ready to go open the store."

Work! I was supposed to be there in an hour. Enduring my five-hour shift at the store suddenly seemed like a colossal impossibility.

"Don't worry," Mom said. "Your dad said he could handle it himself today. I told him you deserved a Saturday off. I thought you might want to see Lucas."

Yes, I thought. Mom was exactly right. I *needed* to see Lucas.

Once I convinced her I was fine and the nightmare was nothing to be concerned about, Mom left me alone. I rummaged through the shelves in my closet until I found my black Vanderbilt sweat suit. After throwing it, and a pair tennis shoes on, I sprinted to the bathroom. I twisted my hair back into the clip from last night, but didn't bother with the loose strands around my face or with make up. I did manage to brush my teeth and use deodorant.

Mom didn't look twice at me as I left, and I knew she thought I was anxious to see Lucas. Which was the truth, but she had no idea why.

I had to make sure he was okay. Healthy. Unharmed.

I'd been to the beach once with Jessie and the girls, and I had a vague idea of where there was an outcropping similar to the one in my dream. I would start there. Find the place and assure myself that it had just been a dream. Then I would call Lucas and come up with some excuse to see him.

I parked in the small, public lot that served this part of the coastline. I shoved my keys and cell into the pocket on the front of my sweatshirt, and walked as fast as I could across the wooden walkway that led to the beach.

Stepping on to the sand, I looked to my left. The rocks were maybe a hundred yards from where I stood, and as I started in that direction, I realized I was walking the same path I'd run in my dream.

The same path I'd seen the woman running on my very first day in Sky Cove.

I picked up speed the further I went, until I was running full force. I fought the urge to shout for him, knowing he wasn't there and my fears were irrational – it had only been a nightmare.

My breathing was rapid by the time I reached the outcropping, my legs burning from the force of my sprint down the beach. The sky was overcast and the cool morning air burned as I pulled it in to my lungs.

Salty, damp ocean air stirred around my face as I bent over, bracing my hands on my knees, trying to calm my heart rate, all the while glancing back and forth, proving to myself that all was fine and that no one had been hurt here as I slept.

I heard the hammering of feet just before I heard his voice.

"Layla!"

Luke sped around the rocks, skidding to a halt when he saw me.

My mind overflowed with questions. I wanted to ask him how he'd known I was here? Had he seen my car? If so, what was he doing driving by the beach this early in the day? Why did his voice ring with the same desperation I felt?

But when I opening my mouth to speak, the only thing that came out was a ragged, "Lucas."

My voice broke when I said his name, and he was there, crushing me in his arms.

His hands traveled from my waist, all the way up my back and neck, and into my hair. The clip that held it all up fell to the sand as my hair tumbled down around his fingers. I snaked my arms around his waist as he buried his face in my hair, thankful for the warm, solid feel of him against me.

My mind was spinning, unable to comprehend what was happening. What had driven us both here, at this precise moment? And why did he seem to feel the same sense of panic and urgency I did?

Gradually, our breathing began to slow, and he pulled back to look at me. The moisture in his eyes caused the tears in my own to spill over, the grief from my dream finally finding an outward expression.

"You're here," he whispered, his eyes locked on mine. "And you're all right."

"Yes," I breathed. "And so are you."

"I was so scared." His face moved even closer to mine.

"Me too."

Gently, so gently it took my breath, he pressed his lips to mine. Tears ran freely down my cheeks at the calm, yet profound assurance that Lucas was unharmed and whole. His mouth moved with such sweetness, and I was torn between the confused misery I felt and the joy that bloomed in my heart.

When he lifted his face from mine, he wiped the wetness from my cheeks with his thumbs. My eyes searched his face in a desperate attempt to find answers. "What's happening Lucas?"

"I'm not sure," he said, his hands still framing my face. His thumbs stroked back and forth on my cheeks and my nerves began to calm a tiny bit. "I used to think I understood it all, but I just don't know anymore."

As uncertain as he sounded, it was clear he knew more than I did. Crazy as it might be, he must've had the same dream as me, and come here searching for the same reasons I did.

"What *do* you know?" I asked.

He kissed me again, this time with vigor, and wrapped me up in the warmth of his embrace. I wasn't sure how long we stood there, entwined with each other, but when the kiss ended, he spoke with a quiet voice.

"It's a long story, Layla. I'll tell you everything I know, but I don't want to talk about it here. I don't think I'll be able to breath easy until we leave this place."

I nodded with major enthusiasm. I couldn't have agreed more.

"Let's walk back up toward the parking lot. I've got a blanket in my truck, and we can find a spot on the beach to talk."

The romance of curling up with Luke on a blanket in front of the sea did not escape me, though something inside me told me the conversation that was coming was more serious than anything I'd ever experienced.

He held my hand as we walked back up the beach, and his fingers gentled on mine the further we moved from the outcropping. It mirrored the relief I felt in my own heart.

Whatever had happened in that dream, Lucas and I were here now. And we were together.

And that seemed more than right.

CHAPTER FOURTEEN

While Lucas retrieved the blanket from the back of his Bronco, I wound my hair in a knot and clipped it back in place. I also placed a quick call to my mom and told her Luke and I were at the beach.

By the time I hung up, he was standing at the walkway with a blanket in one hand and a bottle of water in the other.

"Ready?" he asked.

On the beach we went right, the direction opposite the outcropping. The sun peeked from behind the clouds as we walked, brightening the otherwise overcast morning. When we could no longer see the rocks, we spread the blanket out near the water. The tall grass and evergreens behind us swayed with the breeze.

"Have a seat," he said, gesturing for me to sit down first.

He sat beside me, close enough that our shoulders touched. I pulled my knees to my chest, wrapping my arms around them. Lucas opened the water bottle and offered it to me. I took a few sips and handed it back to him.

We stared out at the ocean for several seconds. The soft rushing sound of the waves soothed my frazzled nerves.

"I'm trying to decide where to start," he said, turning his head to look at me.

"Just start at the beginning."

"It's not that easy." He reached up and ran the backs of his fingers down my cheek. "I don't think my beginning is the same as yours."

"I don't understand any of this," I whispered.

"How did you end up here this morning?"

I opened my mouth to speak, fully intending to tell him everything, but it all seemed so ludicrous when I thought about saying it out loud. How in the world did I refer to the people in my dream? You and me? He and she? Them?

"Lucas, I... it all sounds so – " I stopped, took a deep breath. "Crazy."

"Layla, trust me," he said. "Nothing is going to sound crazy to me."

He was right. Whatever this was, we were obviously both in it up to our eyeballs, given that we'd both done a frantic run down the beach this morning.

"I had a dream," I began. "About you and me. It started off normal, harmless. Just pictures of us at the game last night. Then we were here, walking along the edge of the water. It was still us, at that point, like we really are. But then I was alone on the beach. I was wearing a weird, old dress. And I was running toward the rocks. There wasn't any sound in the dream, but I could hear everything, like it was inside my mind. There were voices on the other side of the rocks. Angry voices. And I knew, somehow, all that rage was directed at you. I tried to scream for you, to stop them, but no sound came out. I couldn't get to you fast enough."

I had to stop there for a moment and close my eyes. I was fighting tears again, though I didn't know why. It was futile, and I might as well just let them fall. He'd already seen me cry.

He seemed to know I wasn't finished, because he didn't say anything. I took a few seconds to get control of myself, and went on.

"As I got closer to the rocks, I heard a beating sound. A loud sort of thumping, like someone being hit over and over again. I couldn't see, but I knew. I knew they were hurting you. I couldn't run fast enough. It just kept on, and I knew I'd failed."

I looked at him then, and I knew he didn't think I was insane. His expression held nothing but compassion.

"I felt it all, every emotion, every fear, all the grief and sorrow. I fell onto the sand and screamed. That's when my mom woke me up. Apparently, I'd shouted in my sleep. As soon as I could get dressed and out of the house, I came here. It was irrational. I knew that, but I couldn't stop myself. I had to come see for myself that nothing awful had happened here during the night. I was going to call you afterward and come up with a reason to see you. I needed to know you were okay."

"How did you know to come here?" His eyes looked at me with such tenderness, such understanding.

"I've been here before," I said. "Once, with Jessie and Marsha and Tiffany, after school that first week. We just walked barefoot in the water. We didn't go down to the rocks. But this morning, after the dream, I knew I'd seen that place before."

"I had the same dream."

His simple declaration almost knocked the breath out of me. I'd known it of course. Why else would he have come here this morning, running to find me and calling my name? But hearing it from him just made the whole thing even more unbelievable.

"What happened to you?" I asked, even though I was afraid to know. "What were they doing to you?"

"I couldn't see that. I saw the same thing you saw." He turned toward me, so that we now faced each other. The wind picked up a bit and blew the loose strands of my hair across my face. He took both my hands in his, holding them on the blanket between us. "It's like whatever happened on the other side of the rocks was a blind spot. I just saw you, running down the beach. I could feel how afraid you were, and I knew it was because of me. And I knew you were running to save me, trying to stop whatever it was that was happening to me. But I couldn't help you."

He lifted our raised hands and kissed the knuckles on both of mine. He took several deep breaths, and I could tell this was as difficult for him as it had been for me.

"I was helpless, Layla," he whispered. "I saw you fall on the sand, and I knew you were defeated, lost, anguished. And I couldn't do anything. I couldn't get to you. I was so scared for you. Scared that whatever had happened to me would happen to you next."

"Oh Lucas," I said, putting my arms around him, letting him pull me into his lap. "I'm so sorry. So, so sorry."

"It's not your fault." He pulled back to look at me. "There's more I need to tell you. Things I've never talked about with anyone. Well, except for my mom."

I moved to sit beside him again. He kept me pressed against his side with an arm around my shoulders. I melted against him.

"When I was eight years old I started having dreams. In the dreams I would see a man, and I knew he wasn't from this time. I knew the dreams were from the past. I didn't see details. The faces were all unclear, and there weren't any specific locations or events. But somehow I knew the man in my dreams was me. I knew I was seeing glimpses of his life, whenever it had been.

"For about three years, I only saw him in dreams. And they weren't scary or unpleasant, so I didn't say anything. But then I started having these visions, or flashes, while I was awake. It was the same man, the same kind of things I'd seen in my dreams, only it was happening while I was conscious. That's when I told my mom."

I looked up at him. I was riveted. Completely captivated by his story. "What did she say?"

"Well, you've met my mom," he said with a smile. "She's not exactly typical, and she's a bit kooky. So, I knew she wouldn't think I'd lost it and try to pack me off to the psychiatric hospital. She started doing research, trying to figure out what these recurring dreams and visions were all about."

"What did she find?" Could there possibly be an explanation for this?

"She told me she thought I was the reincarnation of the man I'd seen in the dreams."

My mouth fell open. Lucas laughed.

"I know," he said. "That was my reaction, too. But, after a while, I had to admit it was the only possible explanation. Mom said she thought the dreams and visions were just a way for me to see bits and pieces of his life, to get to know who he was."

"Did you see me?"

"Not specifically," he said. "At least not then. Like I said, I didn't see details like faces or places. It was all very vague, but yet, very personal too."

"At least not then?" I asked, repeating his words. "Does that mean that you've seen me in your dreams before last night."

He nodded. "The dreams and visions began to get much more definite over the summer. The first time I saw you was July fourth. I remember it because there was a 5K run that day. I was running when the vision hit. That's not unusual. It's actually why I started running in the first place. The visions caught me off guard so often, and I found out if I could relax my mind they'd come then, rather than sneaking up on me. That day, the fourth of July, I was running the 5K. And I saw you... her... running along the beach. And somehow I knew that she was connected to the man I'd been seeing in my visions for years."

Stunned was too mild a word for what I was feeling. I'd read books and watched movies where this kind of phenomenon happened, but never in my wildest imaginations could I have conjured a situation like this one.

Dreams, visions, reincarnation? Had I stepped in to the Twilight Zone? Was Sky Cove some sort of alternate reality?

"You saw me before you actually *saw* me?"

"It was really kind of nice," he said, smiling. "Yours was the first discernible face in any of my dreams or visions, except for my own. And you were beautiful."

How I could be flattered at a moment as serious as this I had no idea, but I was. That Lucas thought I was pretty was both thrilling and astounding.

Just then, something occurred to me. "Wait a minute. You said July fourth?"

"Yes." He looked at me with a questioning expression. "Why?"

"We came here that day," I said. "To Sky Cove. It was the first time I'd been here. We looked at houses. And I saw the same thing. We were driving along the coast. I could see the ocean from the car. I saw a woman running on the beach. I thought she was real, until she plowed right over a family on a picnic blanket, and they didn't even move. It was like she was a ghost. I chalked it up to stress."

His eyes widened. "That can't be a coincidence."

"Do you think I triggered something somehow?" I asked.

He nodded. "You coming to Sky Cove for the first time must be significant. Maybe my visions were waiting for you to arrive before they showed me anything else."

"Be glad you at least had some idea what was happening."

"I can't imagine what this must be like for you. Being thrown into all this with no warning, no warm-up." He kissed my cheek, and I felt his lips move against my skin. "I'm so sorry."

"Not your fault," I said, repeating his earlier words.

The sunlight landed on a patch of rocky sand beside our blanket, and a tiny, shiny green stone and caught my eye.

"What's this?" I asked, reaching over and plucking it off the ground. It almost looked like glass, but it was smooth and frosted, like a gemstone.

"Sea glass," Luke answered. "Sometimes it comes from shipwreck items. Other times it's pieces of broken beer and soda bottles. They'd get tossed overboard by fishermen, and over time the broken pieces get tumbled in the water and tossed against other rocks, until they're smooth like this."

"Interesting." I handed the sea glass to him.

"See how the edges aren't jagged?" he asked, running his finger around the uneven roundness. "Some people try to replicate sea glass with machines and chemicals, but you can tell it's genuine sea glass from the ocean by these small pores. If you look closely, they look kind of like a C-shape." He turned it over in his palm and pointed to a flat area. "Green and brown are the most common colors, but sometimes you find blues and whites or other colors."

"It's beautiful," I said. "It almost looks like an emerald."

"We'll keep it for good luck," he announced with a grin, slipping the green jewel into his pocket. "Since I saw you for the first time right here on this beach."

I liked that thought. And the sea-glass lesson had been a lovely, momentary discussion.

Back to reality. "If you're the reincarnation of this man, do you think I'm the reincarnation of the woman?"

"I think so," he said. "It makes sense, in a weird sort of way."

"What are they trying to tell us?"

"I'm not sure, but I think we've got to figure it out if we want the scary dreams to stop."

"You've had others?" I asked. "Other scary ones."

He nodded. The breeze picked up, causing the edges of the blanket to billow. I leaned closer to Lucas, seeking his warmth. His arm tightened around me for a moment.

"Let's get out of here," he said. "Get out of the wind. We can talk at my house, if you want."

"Okay." I stood up and grabbed the water bottle. "You want to tell your mom?" I wasn't sure how I felt about that. I liked his mom a lot, but this was all so new to me.

"Eventually." He picked up the blanket, shook the sand off the bottom, and folded it. "But not yet. Right now this just seems rather, well, personal, I guess. Like I'm not ready to share it with anybody but you just yet."

CHAPTER FIFTEEN

We found his mother in her office, working away at her computer. She smiled brilliantly when she saw me, jumping up to hug me.

"Welcome back, Layla," she said. Then to Lucas, "There's coffee cake in the kitchen. Be sure and get some for her."

"Thanks, Mom. I'll do that." He kissed her cheek. "Listen, Layla and I have some things we need to talk about. Is it okay if I take her upstairs?"

"To your room?" his mom asked, eyes narrowing.

"Yeah. We won't bother you that way, and if we need to, we can use my computer. We'll leave the door open."

"I suppose I can trust you," she said with a smirk, and it was clear that she did trust him. "But get some coffee cake first."

"Will do."

"You and your mom have a great relationship," I said on the way up the stairs with a piece of coffee cake and a can of Coke. "You didn't really have to ask her about bringing me up here did you?"

He lifted a shoulder. "Probably not. She trusts me, and I never give her reasons not to. But she's my mom, and I don't forget that. So, I ask permission when I should."

No one else on the planet could be like him. There was not another boy alive who thought of his mother this way. It said a lot about Lucas himself, but also about the way Gwen had raised him.

"I love your mom, by the way."

He pushed open the first door on the right and stood back to let me enter. A double bed was against the far wall, and a love seat under the front window. Along the wall opposite the little sofa, sat a rectangular table with a small TV on one end, and a computer and work lamp at the other.

"She loves you, too."

We settled on the love seat with our breakfast, which was now closer to lunch. "The relationship you have with her, it's really great."

"Thanks," he said. "I like to think that we take care of each other nowadays. She's never needed me to take care of her. She's too self-sufficient for that. But it's always been just her and me, so I've felt like the man of the house for a long time. She's done a lot for me, and it's nice that in some ways I can take care of her, too."

We finished the coffee cake in comfortable silence, both aware the talk we began on the beach had to continue. Despite the grave mood, it was pleasant to enjoy the lull and normalcy of sharing a meal.

"I dreamed of you several times before school started," he began, taking our plates and sitting them on the table across the room. "Again, no specifics, just glimpses of us together."

He came back to the love seat and tugged me to his side, his arm resting on my shoulder. He kissed the top of my head before going on.

"After we met, the first time I saw you in a dream was the night before I ran into you at Emerson's Antique Store. That night I saw you standing in the front door of the house.

I was walking up the yard toward you, like I was coming home to you after work."

I gasped. He'd just described the exact dream I'd had. He must've heard me, because he took my chin and turned my face up to his.

"You had the same dream?"

"Yes," I whispered.

"I thought you might've," he said. "But I couldn't be sure. It was possible my dream had just been pointing me there so I'd find you."

"I had a vision," I said. "While we were inside the store. It was more a flash, like you described. When I looked at you through the glass of that paperweight, I saw you as you'd been the night before in my dream. It was just a split second."

He nodded. "I experienced the same thing."

"This is bizarre."

"I also had a vision of you while I was running yesterday, during the meet. I saw myself saying goodbye to you, in the back room of that house. The same place I found that paperweight. I think it may have been the kitchen at one time."

I discovered I wasn't surprised anymore. That he'd experienced the same dreams and visions as me, at the same times, was oddly comforting.

"I fell asleep before the game," I said. "I only meant to chill out for a while. But I fell asleep, and I had the same dream. You didn't want to leave, but you thought it was the only way."

"I wish I knew what I was so afraid of." He scooted near the edge of the love seat and turned to face me. "I wish I knew what the danger to us was. I was trying to protect you by leaving."

"Maybe now that we've figured this much out, the dreams will show us more," I offered.

"I don't know whether to be happy about that or scared to death," he said, a slight laugh in his caramel-smooth voice. "You may get sick of this and decide to leave town."

Strange, but that thought hadn't occurred to me at all. In fact, since meeting Lucas, I'd thought of Nashville and my former life less and less. It was as if Sky Cove had worked its way under my skin without me realizing it. Even with the frightening dreams and unexplained visions, the thought of leaving Lucas was incomprehensible.

"No way," I whispered. "I'm not leaving you."

"Good," he said. "It's probably selfish, but I want you to stay."

I shook my head. "Not selfish."

He smiled then, and leaned forward to kiss me softly. Surprising how quickly I'd grown accustomed to his touch, the way he handled me with care and familiarity.

I thought about his reaction when he'd seen me for the first time at school and smiled. How crazy it must've felt to him when I walked in the building.

"What did you think when you saw me the first time in person?" I asked. "In the lobby, the first day of school. You looked kind of shell-shocked."

He inhaled deeply, a slow smile spreading across his face. His deep brown eyes lit up as his grin encompassed his entire face. He pressed his forehead against mine, forcing my gaze to lock with his.

"I thought, *finally*," he whispered. "Finally she's here."

CHAPTER SIXTEEN

A week had passed since Lucas and I found each other on the beach. A week since I discovered I was the reincarnation of a woman from some previous century.

In many ways, it was almost like it hadn't happened – the dreams, the fear – but I knew it had all been real. I'd had no dreams or visions in the last week, and neither had Lucas. Perhaps our predecessors had decided to give us a break from the intensity of what we'd been shown.

Whatever the case, it was a relief.

My routine with Lucas continued. Literature class second period. A walk to my third period U.S. History class. A quick meeting in the parking lot after school.

And lots and lots of phone conversations in the evenings.

Luke ran every day after school, and, given that he was an honors student, his evenings were taken up with homework and studying, as were mine. But he always made time to talk with me.

I'd had a couple of boyfriends in Nashville, but I'd never felt like a priority to either of them. Lucas's attention made me feel special, and cared about.

We'd agreed to always keep our cell phones handy. I even slept with mine in my hand or beside me on the mattress. Once we discovered that our dreams and visions were happening simultaneously, Lucas said it only made sense for us to be able to call immediately.

He even told me to call in the middle of the night if I had a dream.

He'd been dealing with the reincarnation business for quite some time, and though he was taken by surprise by the specific and frightening nature of our recent visions, he knew that for me it was especially scary.

He said there was no reason for me to be afraid alone, when he was just a phone call away.

Our relationship wasn't exactly public, though after the football game speculation had increased. But nothing about our appearance at school had changed. He didn't move to hold my hand in the hall or the parking lot, and I had a suspicion Lucas wanted to keep some things private.

It also kept me from looking like a total liar to Chris, Robbie, and Lance, whom I'd turned down because I "wasn't ready to start dating".

Today was Friday, and Luke was running in a cross-country meet after school. The host school was in Belfast, a town only twenty minutes away, and my parents agreed to let me drive over and watch.

Not that cross-country was that exciting to watch. I basically just sat near the finish line with Gwen and waited for him to show up. The runners would end their route in the high school parking lot, and several chairs had been placed under the awning at the front of the school.

Gwen settled in to read a book while we waited, and I decided I could also make good use of my time. Luke said he let his mind wander when he ran, that relaxing his mind while running sometimes allowed the visions to come to him in a way that didn't knock the breath out of him.

I figured I might as well try to chill out and see if anything popped into my thoughts. I wouldn't mind something flashing around in there so much if I was expecting it.

The day was overcast, not rainy, but damp and cold, like some sort of anti-sauna. I'd bundled up in black fleece pants and a black turtleneck. Lucas had insisted on lending me one of his Sky Cove X-Country hoodies. It said *Ellis* on the back.

Wearing it thrilled me to pieces.

I lifted the hood, pulling the sides tight around my face and ears, and leaned back in my chair. Ipod headphones went in my ears, and I hit shuffle and tried to relax.

I liked music a lot, and I liked a lot of different music. Lucas said shuffling through the library on my iPod was the equivalent of aural-whiplash.

I leaned back in my chair, closed my eyes, and tried to turn my mind loose.

Plenty of things ran through my thoughts. Of course, Lucas was the star. I thought of school, the football game, the countless phone calls, even that awful dream that guided us both to the beach last weekend. It all kind of flitted across my consciousness, flashing in and out like slides on a power-point presentation.

But there was nothing new. No new pictures from the past, no new emotions from the long dead people who had invaded our present reality.

I was both disappointed and relieved.

Disappointed because as much as it frightened me and interrupted my normal life, I really wanted to know what had happened. I wanted justice or vindication or whatever would make it *right* for the people Lucas and I had once been. I also wanted the dreams and visions to stop. At least the scary ones.

The relief I felt was two-fold. For one, the visions left me ragged and raw, emotionally drained, and it would have been difficult to hide that in front of Gwen. True, she knew about Lucas's reincarnation, and she knew that he'd seen me in his dreams before I came to Sky Cove. But she didn't know about the dreams I'd had, or about what Lucas and I had discovered about ourselves. I was also relieved because Luke wouldn't be distracted by a vision during his run. He could focus totally on his sport, and hopefully come in first again.

I wanted to see him cross the finish line before anyone else and cheer him on as he did.

"You know," Gwen said, breaking the silence between us. "Lucas has a birthday on Sunday."

I pulled the headphones from my ears, a smile spreading across my face. "He didn't tell me."

"That doesn't surprise me," she said. "He never likes to draw attention to himself."

"Which is exactly why he gets so much attention," I added.

She nodded. I wasn't telling her anything she didn't already know.

"Would you come to lunch on Sunday?" she asked. "We'll surprise him with a little get-together, just the three of us."

"I'd love that!"

Instantly, my mind whirled with possibilities for a present. With Lucas, it couldn't be ordinary. It had to be unique, unexpected. But, of course, he wouldn't want anything extravagant. He'd be embarrassed if I placed too much attention on his birthday.

It came to me then, the perfect gift for him. Funny, yet special. Something that would commemorate all that had happened between us.

A group of runners came into sight, just as a sliver of sunlight peeked trough a tiny break in the clouds. They curved around the bend in the road on the hill above the school. One runner broke from the pack, as if a burst of energy propelled him forward toward the finish line.

I knew at once it was Lucas.

Gwen and I cheered as he came down the hill toward the parking lot, faster and faster, traveling further from the rest with every stride, as if he'd saved his last burst of energy for the end of the race. I decided that must've been exactly the strategy, because other runners did the same thing, but with much less effect than Luke.

He crossed the line first, to the cheers of his coaches, his mom, and, of course, me. He only took a moment to catch his breath, down half a bottle of water, and then he came toward us. He kissed Gwen on the cheek, then scooped me up in his arms and twirled me around, as if having me there waiting for him was the best thing in the world.

The heat from his body seeped through the layers of my clothes and warmed me as I wrapped my arms around his neck. He smelled a bit sweaty from his run, but not in a bad way. In a way that reminded me how hard Luke worked for the things that meant something to him.

While watching the world spin as Lucas laughed and twisted around, I thought this must be what falling in love felt like.

Yikes.

CHAPTER SEVENTEEN

Ashley Emerson was as pretty as I remembered, with bright green eyes and the kind of dark auburn hair I'd always wished I had. But mine was just one shade off it seemed... all of the brown without the hint of red. And she was just as friendly today, when I walked into Emerson's antiques after my Saturday shift at String City.

"Looking for anything specific?" she asked.

"Actually, yes," I answered. "And I think I remember exactly where it is."

She waited at the counter while I made my way to the back room. I found what I wanted quickly, pausing for a moment to recall being here several weeks ago with Lucas.

The musty smell once again seemed pleasant and welcoming, rather than old and moldy. I'd wondered if coming back here would feel awkward. It didn't. Instead, it felt comforting, familiar, correct. Of course, my knowledge that this was most likely the place the people in our dreams had lived added to the emotional effect the place had on me.

Still, no vision erupted in my mind, as it had the last time I was here.

I glanced around the room once, trying to imagine it as it had been in my dream, with a wood burning stove and wooden table. The room was small, and though several short rows and cabinets of antiques now filled its walls, as a kitchen the table and stove were probably the extent of what it could hold. I closed my eyes, concentrating on the feel of the room, the air temperature, the scent, the uneven slope of the floor beneath my feet.

When nothing happened, I made my way back up front.

"Interesting choice," Ashley said, ringing up my purchase.

"Sort of an inside joke."

She laughed, a musical laugh that made me feel warm inside. "Well, I hope he appreciates it."

"How long has this house been an antique store?" I asked, hoping to prod just a bit into the history of the place, without rousing suspicion.

"My mother-in-law opened it three years ago," she said. "I've been working since earlier this year, since I married into the family. My husband is Seth Emerson."

"Did anyone live here before that?" I handed her my money.

"Not for several years." She counted out my change. "Seth's grandparents lived here until the early nineties, but then it became difficult for them to maintain, so they moved into a condo for elderly residents in Camden. It sat empty for almost seventeen years before the store opened."

"That's sad," I said. "That they had to leave their home. Are they still in Camden?"

"Patsy is," she replied. "That's my husband's grandmother. Her husband, William, died eight years ago."

William and Patsy Emerson. Strange to think of someone else making their home in this house. Irrational though it was, I had begun to think of this place as always having belonged to Lucas and me.

I thanked Ashley, and promised to come back soon. Making my way out to my car, a thought occurred to me.

There had to be public records of property owners. Maybe even as far back as a hundred years. Of course, I had no idea how to go about finding such records, but they had to be in the courthouse or in some computer database.

If Lucas and I knew that William and Patsy Emerson had owned the house several years ago, could we possibly trace previous owners?

Could we maybe discover the names of the people we'd been seeing in our dreams?

Definitely something I should run past Lucas. But not today. And not tomorrow. At least not until we celebrated his birthday.

CHAPTER EIGHTEEN

Gwen's plan to surprise Lucas was brilliant, if a little complicated. First, she feigned a headache that could only be helped by a specific herbal tea, available only at specialty health food store on the opposite side of Sky Cove from my house.

With Lucas safely out of the house, off to get the tea she needed, she pulled the casserole dish filled with garlic chicken breasts out of the refrigerator and put it in the oven to bake, calling me as soon as she finished. My mom, who was in on the plan, drove me down to Sky Cove Harbor, a tinier version of the harbor in nearby Camden, which was just about the halfway point between my house and Luke's. Gwen met us there, and with only a split second to enjoy the view of the sailboats in and around the harbor, we hopped in her car and raced back to the house. From the harbor, the drive was just under ten minutes, and once there, she retrieved the homemade birthday cake from its hiding place in her office. How she'd managed to bake that and decorate it like running shoes without Luke's knowledge was beyond me.

I'd been put me in charge of decorations, so while she tossed the salad, I set the table. In the center of each plate went a black and gold party hat. I sprinkled the middle of the table with gold confetti and hung a gold foil "18" from the light fixture above.

The chicken came out of the oven just as we heard Luke's Bronco pull up to the house. Buttery garlic wafted through the kitchen.

"Showtime!" Gwen beamed.

"Got your tea, Mom," came his voice from the living room. "Hey, what smells good?"

"Kitchen, Lucas," she called.

He stepped into the room and the two of us shouted, "Surprise!"

For half a second, he seemed stunned, but then his eyes lit up and his beautiful smile began. He eyed the decorations on the table, the cake on the counter, and started laughing.

"You didn't really have a headache, did you?"

Gwen shook her head, laughing too much to answer.

"Happy Birthday," I said, stepping forward to hug him.

He wrapped his arms around me and kissed the top of my head. Gwen moved to embrace us both, then scooted us all toward the table. She insisted Lucas and I sit while she served lunch.

The level of comfort I felt with Gwen continued to amaze me. I found myself, in many ways, anxious to confide in her about the dreams, to have her input on the situation. But, like Luke, I also felt reluctant, as if sharing it right now would be too personal.

At any rate, it was comforting to know we could talk to her and not worry she'd think we'd lost our minds.

My pitiful attempt at singing "Happy Birthday" was made tolerable by Gwen's lyrical voice, and after cutting the cake and stuffing ourselves with devil's food and chocolate buttercream frosting, Gwen announced it was time for presents.

He opened hers first. A new pair of running shoes, apparently the exact kind he'd been looking at for some time. I was certain Gwen had paid a pretty penny for them, but they were the kind of gift Lucas would consider practical and necessary. He'd have them broken in in no time.

I handed him my gift. He opened the card first, which was sweet, but not too sappy, the sentiment inside wishing a happy birthday to someone very special. I thought it struck just the right chord of acknowledgement of our relationship without being overly serious. He found the iTunes gift card inside and smiled. I'd discovered in the last week he did indeed have an iPod, but his playlists were sorely lacking. I'd even told him shuffling through his music was an endless loop of black and white newspaper print.

My heart skipped a beat when he reached for the little box and started unwrapping. Would he think it was stupid? Would he even remember?

But when he pulled the Tequila bottle saltshaker out, his laugh was instantaneous.

"Perfect," he said, laughing and leaning over to kiss my cheek. "Love it!"

"I'm not even going to ask," Gwen said, shaking her head and hopping up to clear the dishes from the table.

I offered to help with the clean up, but Gwen wouldn't hear of it. She insisted that Lucas and I enjoy the rest of the afternoon together. Though it was nippy outside, the sun was out, and we opted for a walk.

At the door, Luke tossed me his X-Country hoodie again, and I pulled it over my head with a grin. I was beginning to think he liked seeing me in it.

I liked being in it.

We walked through the wooded area behind the house, down to the creek that formed the western perimeter of their property. The air was still, the slight breeze doing little more than making a soft rustling sound in the trees. I decided the peacefulness of the moment was right for telling him what I'd thought of.

"I had an idea," I told him, as we walked hand in hand along the creek bank. "Some research we could do that might give us some information about the people in the dreams."

"Let's hear it." His voice was playful, carefree.

I enjoyed this side of him a great deal, and I was glad we'd been able to spend a few days as normal teenagers. The reprieve was a welcome change.

"Well, when I went by Emerson's yesterday to pick up your birthday gift, I got Ashley talking a bit about the house and about her husband's family. Did you know her husband's grandparents lived there?"

He shook his head. "I never paid a lot of attention to the house before, since I didn't see it in my dreams until a few weeks ago. But thinking back, I guess it's been empty as long as I can remember."

"She said they lived there until the early nineties, and then moved to a retirement condo up in Camden. Their names were William and Patsy Emerson."

"Interesting," he said. "I wonder if it's always been in the Emerson family?"

"I think it has been, at least for awhile. And, that's kind of what my idea is." I pulled to a stop, turning to face him. "There has to be some kind of public record, right? Of property deeds and owners? And if we know that William and Patsy Emerson owned the place, couldn't we start there and work our way backwards? Maybe we could find the names of other people who lived there. Maybe even figure out who it is we're seeing in these dreams and visions."

Lucas crossed his arms over his chest, considering.

I went on. "I mean, it might be a long shot to think we could find out who they are, but we might run across something helpful."

"You're brilliant Layla." He smiled at me, his brows drawing together in thought. "The records should be at the courthouse."

"Someone might think we're a bit weird," I said. "Two high school students digging through old records."

"Maybe not." He tilted his head to one side. "I could just say I'm doing some genealogy research. It wouldn't exactly be untrue."

"Well, whenever you have time, just let me know."

We started walking again, this time back toward the house. Lucas remained lost in thoughts. The silence between us was comfortable, and I didn't feel the need to fill it. He'd talk again when he had something more to say.

But the quietness seemed such a change from his jovial mood earlier.

"I wanted to talk to you about how we are at school," he finally said.

"Okay." I felt a bit confused. He hadn't been any different at school than he'd always been.

"I know I haven't exactly been affectionate with you publicly." He stopped walking to lean against the trunk of a large Birch tree. "I've been that way on purpose, I realize I should give you an explanation."

I leaned against a neighboring tree, the branches casting spidery shadows on the ground.

His words had completely lost me.

"Explanation?" I asked.

"It's not that I'm having second thoughts about you, and it's certainly not that I'm embarrassed to be with you." He crossed his arms and eyed me from head to toe. "But this situation we're in is so not typical."

Confused, I looked at him. I had no idea where he was going, nor had I been upset with him for not engaging in public displays of affection.

"The dreams and visions are so clear and vivid now," he said. "Much, much more than they've ever been. Not just the pictures I see, but the emotions I feel. I know it's the same for you – that you can feel what she felt. And this man, he was so afraid, so worried. And it wasn't for himself. It was for *her*. He was scared for her. He knew they were in danger and he wanted to save her from it. He wanted to spare her somehow."

I knew this of course, but I hadn't really stopped to think about how the emotions would affect Lucas differently than me. I may have only been sixteen, but I'd seen enough to know that men – good men, I amended – wanted to protect the people they cared about. Last weekend, on the beach, Lucas mentioned feeling helpless in the dream, afraid that whatever had happened to him would happen to me next. And he'd been completely powerless.

"Lucas, it wasn't real," I whispered. "I know it was scary, but it was a dream."

"I know that in here," he said, tapping his index finger to his temple. He placed his hand on his chest, over his heart. "But in here I know that it did happen. Maybe not to us in the present, but at some point, however long ago, it happened to those people who are channeling into us now."

He was right. I had no doubt that what I'd seen and felt in that dream did indeed occur.

"And I can't help but wonder if history might repeat itself," he said, hands now shoved in his pockets. "I mean maybe not in that exact way, but Layla, if the man and woman we've seen in our visions have been reincarnated through us, who's to say that the bad people, the people who hurt us, haven't also been reincarnated?"

I opened my mouth to argue, then closed it abruptly. It seemed preposterous at first, but once it began to sink in I had to admit it was worth considering. It was crazy enough that Luke and I were now conduits for these people from the past. Why was it any crazier to believe the villains of the story might be channeling into someone else?

I shivered from the thought of it.

"I know I'm probably overreacting, but not being able to protect you in that dream was horrible enough. If something happened in the now and I was helpless to protect you – " he broke off. "That would devastate me."

"It would kill me to not be able to help you, too," I said, moving to stand directly in front of him. "But please tell me what this has to do with you not being openly affectionate with me in public. Which, by the way, I haven't noticed and it doesn't bother me."

Still leaned against the tree, he rested his hands lightly on my shoulders. "I look back on things now, little things that maybe wouldn't seem significant otherwise, and I can't help but wonder if they're connected to all this somehow."

"What things?"

"The incident with Miller the first day of school, for one," he said.

"He did apologize later."

"Yeah, and I'm glad, but even that worries me. What was his motivation for apologizing? Was it genuine?"

"You weren't kidding about worrying."

"Nope," he said. "And there's more. All these guys asking you out, all for the first football game."

I narrowed my eyes at him. Luke hadn't seemed like the jealous type before. Although, I had to admit, thinking he might be a little jealous was kind of exhilarating.

"Not that it's weird that they'd want to date you," he said quickly, reaching out to take my hand. "I mean look at you. And I'm not going to pretend I wasn't a little jealous."

Um... wow.

"You don't have to be," I whispered.

"I take nothing for granted, including your feelings." He smiled. "But it's the timing. Three guys, all in the same week and after we'd started spending time together at school, all for the same event, which just happened to be the day that we had the first disturbing visions. And the fact that Lance asked, too."

"Lance? I thought you guys were friends."

"We are, sort of," he answered. "But Lance, well, he's always trying to *one-up* me. Whatever I can do he's done it already or can do it bigger and better. It's annoying, but I just ignore him."

"You think he asked me out just because it seemed like you and I were getting closer?"

"That sounds so insulting, like I think he wouldn't want to date you for any other reason. And I don't mean it like that." He pushed away from the tree trunk and paced. "But it's almost like the universe was conspiring to keep you away from me. To convince you to choose someone else."

"The universe can forget it." About this I was firm.

He laughed, and the sound of it slid into my ears and under my skin.

Then he turned serious. "Maybe we ought to let the universe think it's winning. Or at least that it's stalled us."

My heart dropped. It must've showed on my face, because he hurried to explain.

"My concern is if I make a claim on you, I mean like a real claim, that you're mine and everyone else better back off, if there is someone out there who's the embodiment of the people who hurt us in that dream – " he stopped and looked right into my eyes. "That it might set them off, aggravate them, spur them into some kind of action."

I didn't like the thought of that. Whatever had happened on the other side of that rock outcropping had been bad enough in my dream, and I'd only *heard* it. I couldn't image experiencing it in real life. The only option was to prevent it from happening.

Our relationship, whatever it was, hadn't been exactly public so far, and I'd been fine with that. So why did the idea of keeping it mostly between the two of us bother me?

"We can't run scared, Luke," I said, taking him by the hand. "As much as I'd like to. I think we have to see it through, find out what happened to the people in the visions."

"You're right, I know. But I think we've got to be careful." He squeezed my hand. "And I just wanted to make sure you understood about the hand-holding and kissing, or lack thereof, at school and around the other kids."

I nodded. "Honestly, Lucas, I'd barely noticed, and wasn't bothered by it at all. I mean, some people are just private about those sorts of things. And I don't mind keeping some things just between us."

I told myself it was foolish to read more into his suggestion of privacy than what he'd just said. It was precaution, pure and simple.

"That's a relief." He kissed the top of my head. "Now when are we going searching at the courthouse?"

CHAPTER NINETEEN

It came to me that night. The insecurity and fear. The stupid, weak, teenage-girl lack of confidence I'd always despised.

It found me as I relaxed in my bed, house quiet, trying to sleep, my iPod ringing last year's playlist. The music reminded me of my last school year in Nashville, and, of course, Adrienne. Or, more specifically, of Adrienne's boyfriend Chase, who had loved her so much he told her it was imperative their relationship remain a secret. He's said no one but them should know the true extent of their feelings. She'd believed him, of course, thinking his desire for secrecy some great romantic gesture. When all the while it had only been a phobia of commitment that had him requesting her silence.

Well, that and a girl from Murfreesboro named Candi.

And this afternoon, Lucas had said much the same to me. The truth of our relationship should not be common knowledge at school. Before our conversation in the woods behind his house, the private nature of our status had been nothing to think about.

Now it was a source of anxiety.

Not that I thought Luke had another girl on the side. No way could I think that about him. But I wondered about the typical I'm-a-guy-which-means-I'm-afraid-of-commitment idea.

Could it be he was having second thoughts about us?

What if my semi-happy card and inside-joke birthday gift had scared him off?

The seriousness of our situation could not be escaped, though it really wasn't of our own doing. Which made it rather difficult for us to have a normal dating relationship. I understood that, and I knew Lucas did too.

I thought back to those first weeks of school, before the dreams started. When the attention he showed me excited me and made me feel special, and the only thing I worried about was whether Miller-the-idiot would strike again or if I'd burn myself on a hot crucible in chemistry lab.

And then something occurred to me.

All that time, when I'd been flattered by Luke's interest, thinking about him and how cute he was and how I'd really like to know him better, he'd already seen me. He'd seen me before school even started. He'd seen my face in his dreams before he'd seen me in person.

It had seemed so sweet, so poignant before, when he described seeing my face in his visions. He'd said I was beautiful. And when he'd told me what he'd thought when he first saw me at school – *Finally, she's here* – my heart had simply overflowed with emotion.

Now I couldn't keep myself from wondering if that in itself would be our undoing.

Could his feelings for me be nothing more than a reflection of his past life? What if all he felt for me were the memories of what the man in the visions had felt for his wife?

And if we succeeded in uncovering the truth about what happened to them, would the connection we'd established come to an end?

Could I be certain about my own feelings? I wanted to think so. After all, I'd started falling for him the very first day of school, before any of this reincarnation madness began. Even though I believed my own feelings to be genuine, what if the strength of my affection for him had more to do with our history and less to do with our present?

What if Lucas was driven only by what his visions showed him? What if he hadn't really chosen me? What if being with me was an involuntary act because of who we'd been in another century?

The questions whirled around and around in my mind, until my head was splitting and my heart aching. It hurt to think of losing the bond Luke and I had. It hurt worse to doubt Lucas. I hated thinking he might've been less than truthful with me today, though I was certain he believed every word he'd said.

When I finally drifted into sleep, the questions remained and the ache in my heart continued. I knew nothing would change for me where Lucas was concerned. Not my feelings and not the way I acted toward him. But I also knew from this point on, I would see everything through the lens of uncertainty that now colored everything.

***

The wet sand was cold on my back, the sky black as tar above me. Around me I could hear the wind whistling, the waves crashing on the rocks, but nothing touched me.

It could have been because I was numb, completely closed off to the elements surrounding me. My mind registered that I should've been uncomfortable, but something in me did not care.

Mere seconds had passed since the horrible sounds from the other sides of the rocks, but it felt like years. The kind of decimation I'd just experienced normally took a lifetime to happen. For me it had happened in a split second.

I wasn't afraid. Not this time. Not like before when I'd been running down the beach. I searched the corners of my consciousness, looking for any hint of fear, but found none.

There was only a cold indifference.

I heard the voices then. The same voices I'd heard before. This time they weren't incensed. The anger I'd heard in them before had been replaced with a stalwart resolve. I knew they were coming for me, and I didn't care.

I was vaguely aware of being picked up from the sand, the wetness making long strands of my hair stick to my cheeks. I did not wonder where they were taking me or what they would do to me. I was beyond worrying about my own safety. What had been done was irrevocable.

They'd taken away the only reason I had to live.

CHAPTER TWENTY

"Are you okay?" Luke's voice was laced with concern.

My cell vibrating in my hand had woken me from the dream, and the depths of despair to which I'd been thrown.

"Give me a second," I whispered, pushing myself up into a sitting position. The air in the house was cool, my skin clammy. I shivered. My alarm clock read 5:30 a.m.

Well, at least I'd gotten most of a night's sleep. I wouldn't miss the thirty minutes between 5:30 and 6:00 a.m. too much.

"I think I'm fine." I pulled my quilt around my shoulders.

"I couldn't stand seeing you that way," he said softly. "So hopeless."

"It sucked from my end, too."

"What was going through your mind?" he asked, though the strain in his tone told me he was afraid of hearing the answer.

"Not a lot," I answered, because it was the truth. "I wasn't afraid anymore. I was numb, resigned. I didn't care what they did to me. My will to live was gone."

I'd never heard Lucas cuss before – just one of the many things that made him so different from other high school boys – but he said a word then that I was quite sure he only said when he was really angry.

"Sorry," he muttered, composing himself quickly. "That's just really hard for me to hear."

"Was really hard for me to feel."

"How do you feel now?"

I took a deep breath, evaluating myself. Even though the emotions of the dream were terrible, I felt marginally better after this one than I had the previous few. Perhaps it was because the fear and grief were gone, replaced by the cold numbness.

"A bit more human than I did after the last one."

"Wish I could say the same." I could hear the tension in his voice.

"Why was this one so bad for you?"

"Because I saw them take you," he said. "And I knew you'd given up. And I couldn't do anything."

"They were beating you in the last dream," I replied. "I know we didn't see it, but that's what it had to be. That's the only explanation for what we heard and the fear I felt."

"I'm pretty sure you're right." He paused for several seconds, as if choosing his next words carefully. Through the blinds on my window the first bits of dawn seeped through, not yet light, but not dark as night. "But I can handle whatever they do to me. What I can't handle is something happening to you."

I was reminded of our conversation in the woods, of his feelings of helplessness and the frustration they caused. And I remembered the questions that had plagued me about the true motivations underlying his feelings for me.

Could his desire to protect me, the need he felt to keep me safe, somehow morph into imagined love?

I decided it did no good to ponder it all at the moment. Not when we'd just been given another piece of the puzzle.

"Let's just try to think objectively for a minute," I suggested. "These are the things we know based on the dreams. These two people were married. They lived in the

Emerson house. Some sort of danger caused him to leave to try and protect her. For whatever reason, that didn't work, because they found him. They took him to the beach and hurt him, maybe even killed him. She tried to stop them, but couldn't. Then they took her somewhere."

"Where would they take her? And why?" he asked.

"And why did they hate him so much they'd try to kill him?"

"I think we better make some time to try to get to the courthouse this week," he said. "The sooner we figure out what happened, the sooner these dreams will stop. I can't stand seeing you like that."

"Same goes," I said, knowing it was the truth. Knowing Lucas had been hurt, or worse, was devastating to me. And I wasn't surprised to know that the woman in my dreams was lost without him. "I don't particularly like knowing that you were being beaten."

"Layla." He stopped for a moment, and I could hear him breathing. "I'm so sorry. I know that's probably not a lot of help, but I really hate you've been dragged into this. When I met you, I thought it would be exciting. Romantic even. I never imagined it would be anything like this."

Whatever my questions concerning Luke's feelings, there was no denying he was a fantastic guy. That he would apologize for something that was not his fault simply because it inconvenienced me spoke volumes about his character.

I couldn't let him shoulder the blame for this situation. "Lucas, this is not your doing, and you know that. You've been as blindsided by it all as I have. Besides, it has been romantic."

"Well, I'm not so sure about that," he laughed. "But I can see to it we have some romance. I still owe you a proper date."

"Luke, you don't have to – "

He cut me off. "No arguments. This Saturday. After your shift at String City. I'll make plans."

My heart tripped in my chest, my concerns not forgotten but put on hold. Didn't matter that I questioned the reality of his feelings for me. I knew *mine* were real, maybe inflated because of our situation, but definitely real, and there was no stopping them when he talked like that.

The love I felt blooming in my heart for him just went right ahead and blossomed without my consent.

"Okay," I whispered.

"I should let you get ready for school."

"Are you running this morning?"

"Probably not," he said. "Not ready to let my mind wander just yet. I'll have breakfast with Mom instead."

"Say hi to her for me."

"Will do."

"See you at school?"

"Of course. And Layla?"

"Yes?"

"I couldn't have imagined a more amazing girl to be a part of all this." His voice was soft and thick with emotion. "Nothing in my earlier visions prepared me for what you'd really be like. I'm truly glad it's you."

I held the phone to my ear like an idiot for a full minute after he'd hung up, replaying his words in my mind.

The blossoming love in my heart multiplied ten times over.

CHAPTER TWENTY-ONE

It seemed the second week of October was National "give a test" week. On Monday, during first period, Mr. Hartley announced that the second chemistry exam would be on Wednesday. Jessie and I made study plans for Tuesday afternoon and evening. In literature, Lucas and I had been reading the assigned collection of Robert Burns poetry, and we learned there would be an essay test over it the following day. We made plans to study that afternoon, when he was finished with cross-country practice. Later in the day, I discovered there would also be a U.S. History test on Thursday.

It was one of those weeks where everything hit at once, meaning the plans Luke and I had to visit the Sky Cove courthouse had to be put on hold until Thursday afternoon.

It felt like a long way off, but the business of Monday and Tuesday kept my mind off it. And also off the lingering questions that had plagued me since Luke's birthday.

At school nothing much changed. Luke still walked with me to third period and sometimes to my car in the afternoons, but he didn't walk as close. Maybe it was my imagination, but it seemed he was putting distance between us, at least in front of the kids at school.

However, we still talked regularly on the phone, so my heart was constantly divided and confused and completely unsure whether to feel happiness or doubt.

The combination was maddening.

On Wednesday, Luke returned to his routine of running in the morning before school, which meant Jessie and I got in one more bit of study time before school started. We'd arrived at school early, finding the chemistry room unlocked. We took advantage of the solitude and quizzed one another over our notes. I wasn't looking forward to the test, but thanks to Jessie, I felt prepared at least.

I was grateful for her once again, for her friendship as well as her willingness to help a science-dummy. A glance at the clock told me the warning bell would ring in a few minutes, so I took a quick restroom break.

I was in and out in less than two minutes, because, really, who enjoys visiting high school restrooms? Even when they're squeaky clean they still smelled like a strange mix of industrial cleaner, hairspray, and cigarette smoke.

As I stepped out into the still-empty hallway, Kara Jennings was waiting for me.

It was obvious I was her target by the way she glared at me from her spot leaning against the wall.

I hadn't met her, not officially, and hadn't really even been around her in a group. She was a senior, so her classes and her lunch period were different than mine. I didn't much want to talk to her now, but I could see no way to escape it, given that we were the only two people in the hall.

But I wasn't going to speak first. No way. If she wanted a confrontation, I wasn't going to be the one to initiate it. Instead, I turned the corner and took a drink at the water fountain.

When I finished, she'd moved to my side of the hallway.

I stopped and waited.

"You must be flattered by Lucas's attention." Her words dripped with contempt.

I thought for a few seconds about how to respond. What was between Lucas and me was *between Lucas and me*. And for many reasons, I would not give her information about the two of us.

But I would also not appear weak or intimidated.

"I'm happy to know Lucas, yes."

I stood straight, squaring my shoulders, not slouching, and not shifting my weight to one leg. Kara might have been taller than me, but that didn't mean I had to cower.

"You should know," she said, her tone condescending at best. "That Lucas is an exceptionally nice guy, and – "

I cut her off before she could continue. "Yes, I do know that."

She narrowed her eyes, clearly ticked I'd interrupted her. I didn't care. This little exchange had barely begun and already she was being catty.

"Plenty of other girls have mistaken his kindness for romantic interest." She crossed her arms over her chest and nodded toward me.

I supposed she must've thought her word was law.

"I'm sure I haven't mistaken Luke's kindness as anything other than it was meant."

"I certainly hope not." She took a step toward me, but I didn't back up. "Luke and I have been together a long time, and this little separation is just a bump on the road to our happily ever after."

I couldn't tell if she actually believed that or if she was just trying to convince herself.

"Don't worry about me," I said, just as the warning bell rang.

I took off toward the chemistry room before she could respond and noticed Jessie standing just outside the door. She'd witnessed the entire thing.

A half smile played on her face, but I didn't feel like celebrating this one. Sure it was a kick in the pants to think

Kara was jealous. But it was another matter entirely to be confronted head-on with it.

"I just want to forget about it," I said to Jessie and I slid into my seat and pulled out my study notes. "I have more important things to worry about right now than Kara Jennings."

Jessie giggled, but in the back of my mind I wondered if what I'd just said was actually true. Luke's worries that the villains from our dreams might have also been reincarnated played through my brain. Every action of every person we encountered was now suspect, and I could see how this could easily become exhausting. Would it now be necessary to analyze and re-analyze every little thing?

And should I tell Lucas?

If I did, would it look like my own jealous attempt to lay claim to him by ratting Kara out?

But if I didn't, might the omission somehow impede what we were trying to accomplish?

I felt the headache begin to throb in my temples, and quickly refocused my mental energy on my chemistry notes. Whatever would happen with the Kara situation could wait one hour, and, it was absolutely imperative we keep up with the responsibilities of our real lives as we sorted through the Swiss-cheese map of our past ones.

CHAPTER TWENTY-TWO

According to Lucas, the Sky Cove Courthouse was a smaller version of the Knox County records department. Yet even with their limited resources, they did have a computer database with records dating back to 1966. That's where we started.

The database had a search feature that allowed us to hunt for names of property owners. This was very useful given that most deed searches required the book number and page number of the deed in question.

By searching for William and Patsy Emerson, we were able to find their deed to the house. From there we found the number of the deed-book for the previous owners.

While Luke typed and searched on the computer, I kept detailed lists of names and dates in a notebook. After about an hour, we were up to our eyeballs in Emersons.

When we reached the 1960's we moved to the "vault" – a small room with floor to ceiling books, shoved into slots with rollers so the enormous books could be pulled out easily. Three moveable ladders slid along the walls, making is somewhat simpler to retrieve the books from the top rows.

It smelled like old paper and dust, and more than a few sneezes crept up on me. The lack of stirring air made the vault feel closed and stuffy. The tile floor was a utilitarian white, dingy from years of foot traffic.

The vault wasn't exactly a happy room.

Lucas went up and down the ladders and handled the books, while I continued my record keeping. The discolored pages in the books crackled, each one harboring the evidence of years and years of smoking within the courthouse vault.

"I can't believe how often this property changed hands," I said, flipping to start the fourth page of notes. William and Patsy had lived in the house since the early 1970's, but before them, it seemed no one stayed there for very long.

"Me either." Lucas pulled another book from near the floor on the far wall. "My guess is the economy caused people to move out of the area looking for work. Commercial fishing was huge in this area in the early 1900's, but if the fishing industry took a hit, people probably moved inward looking for something else. And fishing was difficult on families, with the husband being gone all the time. I've read that a lot of men gave it up because of that."

"Interesting." I found it fascinating. The history and culture of this place was so very different from what I'd known in the south. In Tennessee, agriculture was dominated by cattle and cotton, and in Nashville, where I'd lived my entire life – until this year – everything had been about the music industry.

"And nice that somehow it managed to stay in the Emerson family," I said, even though one brother had sold it to another brother, who'd sold it back to him several years later, and then that brother had willed it to his son, who'd lived there until he moved away and sold it to a cousin, and so on and so on and so on.

In addition to all that, there were also quite a few wills referenced. Those records were in a different set of books, so in my notes I wrote the book number of each one. I figured at some point we'd go through those as well, looking for names or places or anything else that might ring a bell.

I scribbled furiously as Luke read each name mentioned in every deed, doing my best to jot down what little we could learn about the person. We really had no idea what year our dreams were taking place. The only clues we had were the clothing and the condition of the house, which indicated sometime before the turn of the twentieth century. When we pulled the deed from 1923, Lucas thought it might be pertinent to start looking up the wills, since any ancestors or relatives mentioned might have lived around that time.

We discovered that in 1923, Walter Emerson acquired the property through the will of his father, Arthur. Lucas went to the other room to retrieve the book with Arthur's will, then met me back at the conference table outside the vault.

"There are so many names," I said, glancing at the handwritten testament and all the names it included. "And I thought taking notes on the deeds was bad."

Lucas laughed. "I'll see if we can make a copy of the wills."

"That would be a relief."

He was quiet for a moment as we both read the opening.

"Okay, it looks like Arthur was deeded the property from his father, George, after his mother, a.k.a. George's wife Elizabeth, passed away."

I wondered if next we would be discussing who begat whom.

"That was in 1915?" Some of the language was difficult for me to understand, but I did recognize the year.

"Yes. It could be George remarried or moved away," Luke suggested. "At any rate, the property became Arthur's in 1915, then when he died in 1923 it went to Walter."

In my notes I continued my timeline, adding the names Walter Emerson, Arthur Emerson, and George Emerson, as well as the years that Arthur and Walter gained ownership of the house.

"There's quite a bit of personal property listed." Lucas flipped to the third page of the will. "Sort of cool to see what kind of things they felt were important or valuable enough to pass along."

I looked over the list and saw things like *oak table, silver tea set, and wedding rings.*

The jewelry caught my eye. "It says he left his mother's wedding ring to his sister Mary Cutler and his mother's silver tea set to Mary's daughter, Amelia. I wonder why Mary wouldn't have gotten those things from their mother in the first place."

Luke shrugged his shoulders. "Probably because the male child inherited most everything. I suppose that's how it was back then."

"I guess so."

He narrowed his eyes then looked back at the will. "You said Mary Cutler? And her daughter Amelia?"

"Yes." I pointed the place on the paper where I'd seen those names. "Why?"

"There's an Amelia Cutler Light in some of my mom's genealogy records."

"Really?" My mind spun. Could it be?

"Mom has some records she put together just by talking to her grandparents. It gets kind of complicated when you start factoring in siblings and second marriages and all that." He leaned back in his chair, crossed his arms over his chest. "But I went back and looked over her records a few weeks ago, right after we had the first dream about the Emerson house. I was curious if there were any Emerson's in her records. When I didn't see that name, I just discounted the possibility."

"But if the Amelia in your mom's records is the same Amelia in this will, she was Arthur Emerson's niece."

"Seems we have some more research to do," Luke said, rising to take the book to the counter. He paid the clerk twenty-five cents per page to copy the will.

"We should probably talk to your mom," I said as we exited the courthouse and made our way to his Bronco. "I think it's time we told her everything."

He opened my door and I slid in quickly, fastening my seat belt as he made his way around to the driver's side.

"I think you're right. Are you okay with that?"

"Yes," I said. "I think she may be able to help us, especially if you're connected to the Emersons somehow."

He drove in silence for a moment, and I could tell he was deep in thought. I was just about to reach for my iPod, when he spoke.

"Layla?" he asked in a hushed tone. "In your dreams and visions, have you ever seen a child or anything to indicate that these two people had children?"

I shook my head. "The only things I've seen are the things we've seen simultaneously, and there's been nothing that made me think they had children."

"So it's probably safe to assume that if I'm related to the Emerson's, it's not as a direct descendant of the two people in the dreams."

"Probably," I agreed. "I suppose I've always thought the man we've seen was an Emerson. It could be you're related to a cousin or a brother."

"What about her? The wife?" He paused, stopping the Bronco at a traffic light, and looked over at me. "The one who looks like you."

"What about her?" I didn't understand what he was getting at.

"If we figure out who she was, maybe we need to look into her family and their descendants."

"But Amelia was part of the Emerson family." And if Amelia was part of Lucas's family tree, he couldn't also be related to the woman in the dreams.

"I wasn't thinking about me," he said quietly, slowly accelerating as the light turned green. "I meant you."

"Me?"

"Layla, what do you know about your family history? I mean, I know it's unlikely, since you're from Tennessee, but – "

I stopped listening then. Suddenly, I saw what he was suggesting. If he was descended from the Emersons, it could be that I was descended from the family of the woman in our dreams. Was that possible? It seemed so implausible.

I felt my face go pale, the blood draining from my head until I thought I might pass out. I leaned over, propping my elbows on my knees and lowered my head onto my hands.

Luke pulled over to the shoulder of the highway, just before the turn off to White Bridge Road.

"Are you okay?"

I said nothing, still trying to wrap my mind around the possibility. It was far more likely than he thought.

"Luke," I whispered, finding my voice at last. "I'm adopted."

CHAPTER TWENTY-THREE

"How long have you known you were adopted?" Gwen asked.

Luke and I had gone over everything with her, all the dreams, visions, our research at the courthouse. Luckily neither of us had a test on Friday, and my mom agreed to let me stay for dinner, which worked well since Gwen always insisted we eat while we talk.

"I've always known, I guess," I replied. "I mean, I don't remember an event where my parents told me. They just let me grow up knowing."

"How much have they told you about the adoption or your birth mother?" Luke asked, then finished the last bite of his ham sandwich.

"Not a lot," I said. "They always told me they'd answer whatever questions they could, whenever I wanted to know. But I've never asked. It just never seemed important."

"Might be a good idea to ask now, to give us somewhere to start looking." Gwen cleared our plates and set them in the sink. "And speaking of looking, I'll go get my family records, and we'll see where Amelia Cutler fits."

We stayed at the kitchen table while Gwen retrieved her notebook from one of the crowded bookshelves in the living room.

The notebook was a five-subject, spiral-bound protected by a three-ring binder. There was no real organization to it, which fit with the way everything else in Gwen's living room was. It seemed she kept herself organized in the kitchen and her office, but enjoyed randomness in everything else.

"It's just names and stories that I jotted down after talking with my grandparents."

"These are amazing," I marveled, looking from page to page at the things she'd written. Even without a system of order, what Gwen had were priceless treasures of her family history.

"Flip to the back," Luke said. "There's sort of a family tree back there."

On the inside of the back cover, Gwen had written names and years of her family tree. I took out my notes from the courthouse and Lucas and I compared.

There were no common names, in the near past, between Gwen's records and our notes. We looked closely, being careful to look through everything from the courthouse before moving on. Gwen's parents, Richard and Barbara Conner did not appear in our research. Neither did any of her grandparents' names.

However, Gwen's great-great-grandfather was Frank Cutler, and, according to what she had learned, Frank had an older sister named Amelia.

Amelia Cutler.

"The only other information I have on her is that she married a man by the name of Frederick Light," Gwen said. "Apparently, they moved out of the area, and my grandmother – " she pointed toward the name Carrie Cutler Conner – "never really knew her great-aunt Amelia."

"So, what we know is that Amelia Cutler Light was Arthur Emerson's niece." Lucas leaned close, placing his arm around the back of my chair and resting his hand on my shoulder. "And at some point, Arthur owned the Emerson house that you and I have seen in our dreams."

Gwen peered over my shoulder at my courthouse notes. "And Arthur got the house from his father, George Emerson."

"Yes," I said. "But neither Lucas or I have seen anything in our dreams that indicates the two people we've envisioned had children. We think if he's connected to the man in the dreams, it can't be as a direct descendant."

"So we need to find the common link between these people and the man in the visions," Luke added. "Which would be easier if we knew who he was."

"Have you asked them to show you?" Gwen questioned.

"Asked who?" Luke and I said in unison.

"The people in your dreams. The ones who've reincarnated through the two of you."

I took a second to appreciate the fact that Luke and I were having a conversation with his mother about reincarnations and dreams and visions as if it were as normal as taking out the garbage.

"How would we ask them?" Luke asked, his hand rubbing light circles on my upper arm. "I mean, it's not like we can call them on the phone."

"No," Gwen said. "But clearly these people or their spirits are aware of you, since they're speaking to you through the dreams and visions. Perhaps now that you know they're trying to reveal something to you, you could speak to them."

"Out loud?" It seemed crazy, but I figured it wasn't any crazier than the rest of this, so why not. "Do you think they can hear us?"

"It's been some time since I did any reading on reincarnation," Gwen said. "I suppose since Lucas first told me about what he was experiencing. But it seems I remember that many people discussed talking with the spirits, or rather *to* them. Some people described finding a quiet place to express themselves verbally or even just through their thoughts."

"I guess it might be worth a try," Luke replied. "Maybe if we can get a bit of information about who it is we're seeing, we can figure out how we're connected."

"But we still have to know what happened on the other side of those rocks." I shuddered at the thought of it. In my heart I knew. They'd killed him on the beach that rainy night. I just didn't know who *they* were, or why they'd killed him. "And why they hated us so much."

"Knowing who we were is the first step in that." Luke pulled me close, pressing a kiss to the top of my head. "But it's getting late, and I should get you home."

It occurred to me that we'd shifted the way we referred to the people in the dreams. Instead of calling them *he, she* or *them,* we'd begun calling them *us* and *we.* It felt strange, but also right, as if we'd finally started down the right path to end this.

Luke took Gwen's notebook back to the living room, and from the kitchen I could hear keys jingling as he retrieved them from his coat pocket.

Gwen stood from the table and gave me a fierce hug. "You've dealt with all this like a true champion, Layla. I can't begin to guess how difficult it is."

"Lucas makes it easier," I whispered in her ear as I hugged her tightly.

She chuckled. "He has a way about him. But don't sell yourself short. You make this easier for him, too."

***

It seemed a bit too bizarre to talk out loud to the woman from my dreams. Even though I was willing to try most anything to get answers, when the moment presented itself, I couldn't bring myself to say it all out loud.

My parents were long asleep, and I knew they thought I was too. After Lucas dropped me off at home, I'd headed for my bedroom under the pretense of literature homework. In truth, it wasn't homework, but rather a desire for a mental break from everything spinning through my head. I popped my headphones into my ears and set my iPod to play some wordless Mendelssohn instrumentals, and pulled out the small volume of Robert Burns poetry Lucas and I had tested over earlier in the week.

It was lyrical and relaxing, and though I was getting better at reading the Gaelic dialect, the English words scribbled in the margins made the words all the more melodic as I read.

I didn't stop until after midnight. My mind felt peaceful. Not empty, but calm. The house was silent. The wind outside a gentle, serene breeze.

Now was the time.

My mouth refused to work, to allow me to voice my questions aloud. As if that would somehow evoke more than I wanted or needed at this point. Whatever the reason, be it my own fear or something more karmic, I decided not to fight it.

My dream self and I would have this exchange – if there was to be one – via my thoughts.

I imagined I looked like a teenage, wannabe fortuneteller sitting there on my bed, legs crossed Indian-style, eyes closed and breathing deeply. Perhaps the only thing missing was the precise Lotus-meditation pose and some rumbling "ohms" coming from my throat.

But I persisted, refusing to dwell on how ridiculous I must look. After all, no one else was here to see me. In my mind, I pictured the woman from my visions. I chose to remember her as she was in the first dream, happy and smiling, as she waited for her husband to come home to her. I focused on the feelings I'd felt – elation, contentment, harmony. In my mind I called out to her, seeking to somehow link my mind to hers.

I let the questions run through my consciousness. *Who are you? What happened to you? Who hurt you? What do you want us to do?*

As the questions roamed inside me, images from the other dreams flashed behind my eyelids. The despair of watching Lucas leave in order to protect me. The fear as I ran down the beach, hearing him being beaten. The cold, numb, resignation I felt as I was carried off the beach by the same people who'd hurt him.

Strangely, I didn't feel afraid or sad. I felt empowered by the fact that for the first time I was being proactive, and not just waiting for another vision to cut my legs from under me.

I wasn't sure how long I sat there, thinking all the things I wanted to know, but at some point whatever trance-like state I'd entered waned, and I slowly opened my eyes.

Exhaustion came then, and I took the iPod from my ears and laid it aside. My pillow felt softer than usual, and my bed seemed to welcome me like a beloved relative.

The sleep that claimed me was sound and complete, and for a long time I rested dreamlessly. Even from my unconscious state, I was thankful for that.

When the dream began, I knew immediately it was different. Instead of seeing a scenario played out like a movie, there was only sound. Narration. Storytelling.

The voice rang in my ears, a lower, more mature version of my own. And when she spoke, though she spoke of terrible events, her voice soothed me.

In the autumn of that year, they came for him. They said he was a murderer, and accused him of vile and repulsive things. The townsfolk were made to believe that he had done those unspeakable things to her. But he could not have done that. It was not in his nature. He was good and kind and charitable. But no one would believe us. His innocence was doubted by all. The one who sought to destroy him convinced everyone that he was a danger to the town, and assembled a band of vigilantes. When they killed him, they believed they were justified. The other people of the town thought he ran away out of guilt, out of fear of being caught and punished. But I knew the truth. I had heard it all. And they used it to destroy me too.

Cryptic words that only aroused more questions in my mind. But at least I had an idea of what had happened. He was accused of a murder he did not commit. But for what reason? And why did someone seek *to destroy him*, as she'd said?

So I asked. In my mind, I forced the thought. *Why did someone want to destroy him?*

Her answer was swift and succinct. And it was the last she would say to me tonight.

Because he wanted me.

CHAPTER TWENTY-FOUR

The dream didn't wake me, I realized when my alarm went off. And I wasn't emotionally ragged as I usually was after one of the dreams. Perhaps I felt better because last night hadn't been a "show and tell", but rather a conversation of sorts.

I should call Lucas. I reached for my cell phone, but didn't dial just yet. Instead, I grabbed my backpack from beside my bed and pulled out the tablet containing my courthouse notes. I remembered her words almost verbatim, so while they were still fresh in my mind I wrote them down. I also jotted the questions I still had. Who wanted to destroy him? Who had been murdered? And what had happened to her after her husband had been killed?

I reached for my phone, but it vibrated before I could push the first button.

"Tell me about your dream," Luke said when I answered.

"She talked to me," I answered. "I didn't see her. I didn't see anything. I just heard her voice."

"He talked to me," Luke added. "Same thing. No pictures, just words. What did she say to you?"

"I wrote it down, hang on." I re-opened the notebook and read it back to him.

"Almost exactly what he said to me, except from his point of view."

"It wasn't scary," I said. "And it didn't wake me up."

"Me either."

I could hear him breathing deeply, and I knew he was considering what to do next. Generally, after a dream, he didn't like to run in the morning, since the possibility of another vision was so great. It was always comforting to arrive a bit early at school after a dream, just to have a moment together. It gave each of us some peace of mind to be in each other's presence afterward. But today was Friday, and he had a meet this afternoon. He needed the running time.

And besides, neither of us had been disturbed by this dream.

"You should run this morning," I finally said. I knew the need he felt to protect me, and he would do it even at cost to him. "I'm fine."

"Are you sure," he whispered. "I'm sure I'll be fine this afternoon, even if I don't run this morning."

"Luke, you can't put your real life on hold all the time." I closed the notebook and returned it to my backpack. "And this dream wasn't frightening. It was informative. So take your morning run. We should probably both take some time to think about it all before we start trying to pick it apart."

"I hate not being with you after one of these episodes."

I smiled at his attempt to talk himself out of running. It was sweet and very, very indicative of who he was. But it also reminded me of the questions I harbored concerning Luke's true motivations, and I wondered once again if the strength of the feelings he seemed to have for me stemmed only from the memories he had from our past life. Did it even work that way? Did he have the man's memories? I knew I'd experienced the woman's feelings in my dreams, but I didn't have any memories other than the one's she showed me. And outside of the visions, I didn't *feel* like her. But Luke had been having these visions for a long time. Could the love he felt for his wife long ago have somehow carried over, making him believe he felt something for me when it wasn't actually there?

And if his feelings were some kind of carry-over, did that make them less real or more real? Thinking about it was fast giving me a headache, so I forced myself to stop.

"Go run, Luke," I said.

"If you're sure." The sound of his gentle laughter made me smile.

"I'm sure. I'll see you in literature."

"Counting the minutes," he replied. "Be safe."

My heart twisted and lurched as I hung up the phone. It was absolutely impossible not to be in love with Lucas Ellis. No way could I stop the runaway train I was on, not even with the fears and concerns I had concerning the true source of his feelings.

It was both a miserable and ecstatic place to be. I decided the most prudent thing I could do was to enjoy each moment with Lucas, and not wonder which one would be the last.

Yeah, like I wasn't going to worry.

***

I sloshed through the puddles of water in the parking lot, thankful that at least the rain had let up enough for me to walk into the building without getting soaked. In my back pocket, my phone vibrated just as I pushed open the front door.

It was a text message from Lucas. This was new. He usually just called. I flipped open my phone and pressed the button to read.

It was part of one of the Robert Burns poems from our literature assignment.

Long have we been parted, Lassie my dearie;
Now we are met again, Lassie lie near me.
All I have endured, Lassie my dearie,

In thy arms is cured, Lassie lie near me.

I knew people must've been staring. I hadn't even moved from the doorway, and students coming in had to walk around me. But as I read those words, and thought of all Lucas and I had learned about our past and about each other, Burns' poem took on new meaning. We *had* been separated for a very long time - though neither one of us had realized it - and there was a definite sense of comfort in finally being together again.

And Lucas had read that poem and thought of me. Had entered the words into a text message completely spelled and punctuated. My heart expanded painfully in my chest.

Just then my phone buzzed again. Another incoming text from him.

When I'm with u, u cure the bad stuff. Don't 4get. Proper date 2morrow nite. Already ran it past ur parents. Love, Lucas

Wow. Just wow.

I closed my phone, making sure to keep the messages to re-read later, and pushed through the sea of people in the lobby. I hoped to find Jessie already in the chemistry room. A tap on my shoulder caught my attention before I got out of the crowd.

"Hi Layla." It was Todd Miller's voice.

I didn't cringe, but I did mentally roll my eyes. I wondered why I was one of those people who always had to be polite, no matter what.

"Hi Todd."

"Um, listen, I wanted to talk to you." He walked toward my hallway, motioning for me to follow. The fact that I had to go that way anyway made it impossible for me to come up with an excuse.

"What about?" I asked when we stopped just outside the lobby. He wore too much cologne, and it reminded me of being at one of those department store cosmetic counters where people got carried away and sprayed multiple samples.

"Well, I know you've been hanging out with Lucas," he began. "But I wasn't sure just what the situation is with you two. I mean, Kara's been telling people she and Luke are talking again, and they do have a couple of classes together, so I guess it's possible."

My chest constricted at the mention of Kara's name. Kara, who'd made her jealousy and her intentions clear to me two days ago. Kara, who was tall and slender and blond and beautiful.

And, Kara, who I was quite certain had *not* just received a text message with a love poem from Lucas.

I considered it a victory.

"I'm not sure where you're going with this," I said, glancing around to make sure no one was eavesdropping. "What difference does it make what the situation is between Lucas and me? And why do you care?"

"I just still feel bad for how I acted the first day of school," Miller said. "And Kara, well, she can be pretty mean sometimes. And, I guess I also thought, if you and Luke were just friends, maybe you might, I don't know, think about going out with me sometime."

Oh geez. During two years of high school in Tennessee, I'd been asked out exactly twice. Now, in less than a month, I'd been approached by four guys. Five if I counted Zack's thwarted attempt at the locker the week of the first football game.

"Wow, Todd, I'm flattered, really." I stopped, took a second to think about what to say next so that I didn't stumble over my words. "But I think maybe we should just stick to being friendly with each other and living down the incident from the parking lot."

"Yeah." He stuck his hands in the pockets of his jeans and looked down at the floor. I could see a small smile on his face and he laughed. "I guess there would be talk if we dated too soon after that."

"I appreciate the apology," I said. "And the warning about Kara. Although it's really unnecessary."

"No problem." He nodded. "See you around."

Then he walked back to the lobby and strode down the other hall just as the warning bell rang. While I headed down the hall toward chemistry, I pulled my phone out of my pocket and read Luke's texts again.

CHAPTER TWENTY-FIVE

Jessie came in late to first period. Fifteen minutes into chemistry she trudged in, wet and frustrated after a flat tire on the way to school. Mr. Hartley hadn't finished our tests, which was disappointing, but on the flip side, it looked as if the chapter on balancing equations might click a bit more for me than the last chapter.

During second period, Lucas refused to tell me anything about the plans he'd made for tomorrow night. And even though my curiosity was huge, I liked the idea of a surprise. I resisted, but not without effort, the temptation to pull my cell phone out during literature and re-read Luke's text messages. I did, however, whisper a *thank you* to him, just as Mrs. Chadwick began the class. Though it would've been far too embarrassing to have a conversation about the texts and how they'd touched me, it seemed far too rude to say nothing. So, I found a way to acknowledge his thoughtfulness that didn't require a lot of talking.

His answer to my *thanks* was a grin and a wink.

Mrs. Chadwick returned our Robert Burns tests first, and I smiled when I saw the A's on both my paper and Luke's. The bookworms compared test scores, all of them seeming pleased. The cell-phone addicts each took a look at their grades then quickly put them in their bags. I surmised they either were not happy with their grades or just didn't care.

We learned that our next reading assignment, which was due to be completed by this time next week, was Leo Tolstoy's novella *The Death of Ivan Ilyich*. I struggled not to have a bad attitude. I'd read lots of books, many of them classics, but until now I'd managed to avoid Tolstoy. I'd stuck to J.D. Salinger, Louisa May Alcott, Mark Twain, and the like. It was probably fear that kept me from attempting *War and Peace* or *Anna Karenina*. Thankfully, our assigned story about a forty-five year old man dealing with his impending death was only one hundred thirty-four pages. Perhaps it was a good introduction to the works of the great Russian novelist.

At any rate, I decided the reading would be a nice distraction from whatever our past selves had in store for us next. I was sure to need a few moments of something else during the coming week.

"I'll call you when I get home from the meet tonight," Lucas said as we walked toward my U.S. History class.

"And tell me how you came in first again?" I teased.

"And tell you how the team did," he corrected with a chuckle.

We stopped beside the door. I leaned against the wall, and Lucas did the same, as we got out of the way of the hall traffic. For a moment he just looked at me, in the way he had that made me curious and weak in the knees at the same time.

I was pretty sure anyone looking too closely at us would see there was more to Luke and me than friendship. But for whatever reason, at this moment, Luke didn't seem to mind.

"Mr. Radnor sent me on an errand during first period," he began. "I took some papers to the front office for him. I ran into Jessie as she was checking in."

"Yeah, she had a flat on the way to school."

"She mentioned you and Kara had words the other day. I think she thought I already knew."

Holy crap. I'd meant to tell him. I really had. But with everything else that had gone on – our search for information at the courthouse, the discussion with Gwen that followed, our communication with the people from our past – I'd just forgotten about it until this morning.

"It's not important, Luke," I said, my voice soft as I stepped closer to him. "I'd forgotten all about it until today anyway."

"I should've seen this coming." He tilted his head, bringing his face closer to mine. "Kara's got a nasty streak."

"I kind of got that."

"Do you want me to talk to her?" he asked. "Tell her there's no chance she and I are getting back together?"

Just hearing the words come out of his mouth sent chills over my entire body. Not that I'd thought he wanted to be with her, but to hear him say *no chance* was a thrill beyond description.

"Luke, that's sweet." I gave him my warmest smile. "But I think it might make things worse."

"I hate thinking about her bothering you."

"What happened to not wanting to set off anyone who might possibly be channeling the bad guys?" It was only a half-joke, but Lucas laughed anyway.

"If it happens again, will you tell me?"

"Of course," I answered. "I meant to tell you this time. I just forgot."

"She's not right, you know." He leaned even closer, keeping our words from anyone else's ears. "Kara and I rarely speak, unless you count polite hellos. And there is no happily ever after in our future."

I smiled, too moved by his words to talk out loud. A part of me fought and clawed to keep my heart from tripping even further down the slope of love. I knew it was futile, but I fought nonetheless.

And continued to lose the battle.

"Talk to you tonight," he said.

***

When I walked into the cafeteria for lunch, not only was I met by the lovely smell of unseasoned steaming broccoli, I found Jessie and Marsha, along with Robbie and Chris, huddled over something at our table. The four of them saw me at the same time, and Jessie scrambled to shove something underneath her lunch tray. They looked as guilty as kids caught sneaking into the cookie jar.

"Give it up," I said, pulling out a chair and dropping into my seat. "I know you're all up to something."

"It's nothing," Marsha responded, shaking her head.

"Yeah, it's just stupid," Jessie offered. Her eyelids lowered and she pulled her lunch tray closer to her.

Clearly, it was not just something stupid. I'd gotten to know Jessie well enough that I could read her face.

"I can tell that it's not nothing." I leaned my elbows on the table and looked at each of them. Jessie still looked down at her tray. Marsha bit her lip. Robbie drummed his fingers on the table, and Chris feigned an interest in something on the other side of the room. "You might as well spill it."

"Somebody's idea of a joke," Jessie said, her breath coming out in a disgusted huff.

"What's under the tray, Jess?" I asked.

"Oh, just show her," Marsha blurted. "It's not like it means anything."

Jessie's eyes cut toward Marsha. She nodded, then pulled a piece of paper out from beneath her tray.

She slid it across the table toward me, while the guys started a conversation about cars. Apparently, whatever was going on, they wanted no part of it.

"This was on our table when we got here." Jessie's voice dripped with apology. "Robbie said there's more in the lobby and on the bulletin board outside the front office."

It took a moment for my brain to process the picture in front of me. It was black and white, as if it had been run off on a copy machine or printed from a laser printer. But even without color, I could see Lucas was in a tuxedo, smiling brilliantly. Other tuxedo-clad boys dotted the background of the photo, along with girls in fancy dresses. Prom. It must be a picture from the prom.

And then it registered. The girl who was wrapped in Luke's embrace was Kara. They were dancing, her head tilted back as if in laughter. And they looked so happy together.

Ugh.

I took a deep breath, reminding myself I had to be careful how I reacted. First of all, I would *not* act the role of jealous girlfriend. That would be playing right into Kara's hands. Second, people could speculate all they wanted, but the official status of my relationship with Luke was not to be common knowledge. For several reasons - not the least of which was that the two boys at the table, pretending not to pay attention, had asked me out and I'd said no on the basis of not being ready to start dating.

Then there was the whole possible-reincarnation-of-the-bad-guys issue to consider.

Keeping my cool was imperative.

"You're right. Stupid." I tossed the picture back on the table, with as much nonchalance as I could muster. "I don't know what they were trying to accomplish, but whoever put that there was obviously reading way to much into my friendship with Lucas."

Jessie picked up the paper, ripped it in half. "They, and by *they* I mean Kara Jennings, were trying to make you jealous. It had to be her who put it here. I mean, remember how she acted in the hall the other day?"

"She's obviously not over Lucas," I said. "And I can't blame her. He's a great guy. But if it's meant to work out between them, it will."

Gag! Choking those words out without gagging felt like the greatest accomplishment of my life.

"I thought you and Luke were pretty much an item," Chris said.

So much for pretending not to listen.

"We're friends. We study together for literature class sometimes."

"Come on," Jessie replied. "There's more to it than that. I can tell by looking at the two of you."

"And I heard you went to see him run up at Belfast last week." This from Robbie.

Okay, so downplaying things didn't seem to be very effective. I needed another strategy, fast.

"Look guys," I said, lowering my voice. "I don't want to get my hopes up, okay? I mean, Lucas is a great guy and I like him. But I realize I'm new here and that he and Kara have a history. I'm just enjoying getting to know him and trying not to have expectations."

It wasn't as hard to lie as I thought it would be. Probably because not all of it was a lie. I was *trying* not to get my hopes up too high, although I knew deep down it wasn't working. And I was *trying* not to have too many expectations. Trying, but not succeeding.

And pretending to be semi-worried about Kara wasn't too difficult. She was popular and beautiful - two things I'd never been. But it was also hard to picture Luke with her. She was so different from him and his kind, selfless ways. She was like the anti-Lucas.

"And so you're trying to be happy just being friends with Lucas?" Marsha asked this as if I'd just said I was trying to defy gravity.

"I *am* happy with the way things are." There, that was not a lie. "Like I told Kara the other day, I haven't mistaken Luke's kindness as anything other than it was meant."

Through the cafeteria doors, a group of seniors passed by. During the lunch period, each grade changed classes on a different schedule to avoid overcrowding in the lunchroom. Lance walked in front, followed by a trio of girls. I knew Corey and Will wouldn't be far behind. I turned my head from the door, not up for one of the friendly waves I knew Corey would give.

My phone vibrated in my back pocket. For a person who didn't particularly love text messaging and didn't use it all that much, three texts before lunch was a record.

I opened the phone, careful to be discreet and keep the others from seeing the message and who sent it. It was from Luke.

Ignore the pics. Another Kara stunt. U r the girl of my dreams.

Oh good grief. How in the world was I supposed to keep my heart even the tiniest bit safe when he said stuff like that? Of course, it wasn't just pretty words. He was speaking literally. He did dream about me.

I closed the phone, returned it to my pocket, and pushed back from the table. I had to give the girls some sort of explanation. I supposed it was an unwritten rule that texts received in the company of friends had to be explained.

"A reminder about literature," I said, not telling them for sure it was from Luke. "We got a new reading assignment today. I'm going to get some lunch."

Walking toward the sandwich bar, the tingling sensation began, moving up my spine and across my skin. Words moved through my mind, random at first, but then sliding into place.

It happened quicker this time because I didn't fight it. I'd ceased to be surprised anymore, and whatever haywire thing was happening in my brain just might be connected to all this other supernatural stuff plaguing Luke and me.

The phrase formed with clarity before I even lifted my lunch tray from the stack.

Even if I have to kill him.

For a moment it seemed my heart stopped, and the lunch tray almost slipped from my hands. But I reigned myself in, forcing myself to look normal. If whoever was having those thoughts was in this room, the last thing I wanted to reveal was that I was aware.

Behind me, someone cleared a throat. Right. I was holding up the line.

I grabbed a chicken salad sandwich on wheat bread and glanced behind me. "Sorry."

"No problem." It was Phoebe, the girl from the hallway the other day, who always seemed to be so unhappy.

"Just distracted, I guess," I muttered. "Aren't you a senior? How come you have lunch with us?"

"Glitch in the scheduling." She eyed the broccoli and decided to pass. "Since I have art last period, I'm in senior English this period. It's a small class, so we all come to lunch early."

I nodded, reaching for a bag of corn chips.

"I saw the pictures." She picked up a banana. "Told you people here suck."

I was sure she felt that way. Which was awful. Was anyone *ever* nice to her?

I smiled at her. "Well, I don't think *you* suck. Hopefully you don't think I do either."

She just shrugged. "Kara Jennings seems to hate you, so in my book that's a point in your favor."

I glanced back at the table, at the paper lying in the center, and thought about Kara Jennings.

Something was definitely brewing at Sky Cove Senior High.

CHAPTER TWENTY-SIX

Corey met me in the front lobby as I left school that afternoon. He was one of Luke's closest cross-country buddies, and though I wasn't certain, I thought he might've been the only person Luke had confided in that we were more than friends.

"Hey Layla," he said, catching up with me as I made my way through the crowd toward the front door. "Lucas wanted me to tell you Coach Roberts sent him to pick up a case of bottled water before we leave."

"Okay, thanks." And wasn't it just like Lucas to think of me? It wasn't like we had some kind of standing date at the end of each day to see each other in the parking lot. But it was so like him to be considerate enough to let me know why he wouldn't be there today.

"I'll walk you out, if that's okay with you." He pushed the door open and held it for me. "Luke was kind of worried after what happened today with those pictures."

I smiled. Luke's protective gestures were so endearing.

No one gave us a second glance as we made our way through the parking lot in the misting rain. As much as I'd gotten used to the attention, it felt nice to not have eyes watching me as I walked to my car.

"Tell Luke, I said good luck," I said as I reached my car. "And good luck to you, too."

"Thanks. We'll be headed out as soon as Luke gets back with the water."

I reached into the front pocket of my backpack, but as my hands closed around my keys, I saw my door was already unlocked.

Odd. I was always so particular about locking my doors.

"That's weird. My door's unlocked."

I leaned down to look in the window, and Corey stepped around me to do the same.

"Anything missing?" he asked.

"Doesn't look like it." I pulled the door open for a closer look. "I must've just forgotten to lock it this morning."

Which was a definite possibility, since I'd still had last night's dream on my mind when I arrived at school.

"Um, Layla I think I ought to ride with you."

"What?" I turned back around to face him.

"Well, Luke confides in me some, and I know he's been kind of concerned about the things that have been said and done. And after today, with the pictures, it's obvious somebody's messing with you."

"It was a stupid prank," I argued. "That's all."

"Even still, I think Luke would appreciate it if I rode with you."

"But you have to leave for the meet."

"I'll call Will, have him follow us and pick me up at your house."

"How are we going to explain that to Will?" I asked. "If Luke's confided in you then you know the two of us want to keep a low profile."

"I'll tell him you had some car trouble." He shrugged his shoulders. "And I thought Luke would want me to be sure you made it safely home. It isn't really untrue, and Will realizes there's something between you guys."

"Please don't make a big deal out of this to Lucas," I said. "I don't want him distracted when he runs."

"I won't say a word, until after the meet."

"All right then," I agreed. "Call Will."

Corey pulled his cell from his pocket and made his call while I loaded my backpack in the back seat. Once we were both in the car, I cranked the ignition.

Loud, heavy metal music I did not recognize burst from my speakers, making both of us jump. I slammed the off button. Eyes dropping to the console, I saw the CD I'd been listening to this morning lying loose between the two front seats.

That CD had been in my stereo when I got of the car before school.

"Someone's been in here," I whispered. Thank goodness the car was still in park, because I was shaking too much to drive.

"You're sure?" Corey said.

I nodded, picking up the CD and showing it to him.

"I was listening to this. I left it in my stereo." I pointed at the radio dial. "And whatever that was, it wasn't anything I chose myself."

"Let's see what station it is," Corey suggested. "Might give some place to start."

"Start what?"

"Figuring out who got in your car."

The shaking began to subside and I took several deep breaths. Would it even do any good to report it to the principal or the school resource officer? Nothing missing or broken. There was no evidence of wrongdoing, other than the music. Would they believe someone had been in my car?

"Why don't you let me drive?" Corey asked.

I nodded and got out of the car.

We switched spots and Corey took off. Halfway to my house the rain picked up and he turned on the wipers.

The windshield smeared and clouded, rather than clearing.

"What in the world?" I said, not really expecting an answer.

Corey tried them twice more, with no success. The smearing just got worse. He didn't say anything. Just rolled down the window and leaned his head partially out, peering through the rain and slowing the car to a crawl. Traffic in my subdivision wasn't heavy, which worked to our advantage, as he was able to creep his way down the street and over to the next block. He turned in to my driveway just as Will pulled up.

Corey was out of the car in a second, inspecting the wipers on my car, seeming oblivious to the rain.

"Looks like Vaseline," he said.

"You're kidding."

"Look, I'd stay and help you clean it up, but I've got to get going," Corey said, looking at Will waiting in his truck. "You can probably get this off with a rag or a squeegee."

"I'll take care of it. You go."

He started toward Will's truck, but turned back around.

"Layla, Vaseline on windshield wipers is a harmless prank sometimes. But putting it there on a rainy day, well, that sort of smacks of more than a practical joke."

"Don't tell Luke."

"I can't keep this from him," he said. "And neither can you."

"I know that," I corrected. "Just don't say anything until after he runs, okay?"

When he looked like he might argue, I took a step closer.

"I'm home safe, my mom's here, and my dad will be home later. I'm not going anywhere. You can tell him after the meet, and he can come by here and we'll talk about it."

He nodded once and hurried to the curb. I looked at my cell phone and realized the entire episode, from the blaring music in my car to this moment had been less than ten minutes. Surely the two of them would make it back to school in plenty of time to get on the bus.

Looking at my car, I took a deep breath, trying to decide what to do. Cleaning that mess from my wipers and windshield was first on the agenda, but after that, I decided to make a list.

Luke's theory about the villains in our visions being reincarnated just might hold more water than we'd thought.

***

Getting the Vaseline off my windshield turned out to be more of a job than I'd imagined. I scraped a lot of it off with my ice scraper, but afterward it still took almost an entire roll of paper towels.

I kept waiting for Mom to come out and inquire about what had happened. I hated the thought of being untruthful with her, but how could I tell her someone had gotten into my car and sabotaged my windshield wipers? She'd be on the phone with the principal immediately, followed by a call to the police. I couldn't explain to her that Lucas and I were dealing with forces beyond what the police could deal with, and the Vaseline on my wipers may well have been the result of an evil older than all of us.

When I went inside, I wasn't totally satisfied that I'd removed all the slime, but it was enough I could see. And the wipers were clean. I made sure of that.

In the kitchen, I caught the scent of fresh pastry and some kind of berries, just as Mom pulled a pie out of the oven. And there were chocolate chip cookies cooling on the counter. No wonder she hadn't come outside to check on me. She'd been busy baking. I thanked my lucky stars.

"Dinner may be a bit later tonight," she said over her shoulder. "I was in the mood for pie and cookies, so I haven't started dinner yet. Did you know Maine blueberries are in season?"

"No problem." I grabbed a cookie, and leaned over to smell the fresh-from-the-oven blueberry pie. Butter, sugar, and blueberries make a lovely aroma. "I've got some things to work on before we eat anyway."

"Lucas called this morning." Mom's words halted me on my way to the stairs. "Asked if it was all right to take you to Camden for dinner tomorrow night."

Camden. Nice.

"He hasn't told me where we're going. He wants to surprise me."

"Oops." She sat the pie on the counter and turned off the oven. "I'll say no more, then."

"He might be here for dinner," I added. "He said something about coming by when he got back from his meet."

And I knew after Corey told him about the business with my car, he'd be here as soon as he was back in town.

"That's fine, honey. We'd love to have him."

I made my way to my room, thoroughly enjoying the taste of warm milk chocolate. Being a Friday, I didn't have a lot of homework, so I decided to put it off. Instead, I pulled out the notebook that held my notes from the courthouse and last night's dream dialogue, and flipped to the back section.

I started by jotting down descriptions of the dreams and visions Luke and I had experienced. I included not just places, times, and events of the visions, but also how I felt, before, during and after. I figured the more information we had in one place, where we could look and reflect, the more we might be able to glean from it.

After I recorded the dreams and visions, I started a timeline. It began on July fourth, noting that it was my first visit to Sky Cove, as well as the first time Luke saw my face, or any discernible face for that matter, in one of his visions. I continued on through last night's dream, the pictures scattered around school, and the tampering with my car.

A garlicky, tomato-ey scent wafted up from the kitchen at the same time I heard the crunch of tires in the driveway. His meet had been in the next town, only about 15 miles away, so he was back in town quicker than usual. I flew down the stairs, throwing my backpack into the home office on the way, wanting to catch him outside.

This was not a conversation we needed to have inside within earshot of my parents.

CHAPTER TWENTY-SEVEN

I thanked my lucky stars the rain had stopped, as I pulled the door shut behind me and stepped onto the porch. Luke leaned against his truck – still in his running shorts with a Sky Cove hoodie on top – looking at the ground.

And wow. Didn't his legs look great? Yum.

"Don't keep things from me." He didn't look up as I walked toward him.

"Luke, I wasn't keeping it from you," I said, avoiding a puddle as I stepped to lean beside him against the Bronco. "You know that."

"You told Corey not to tell me."

"Until after you ran," I corrected. I touched his arm and he turned his head to look at me. "I was safe at home, and there wasn't anything you could do other than worry. I didn't want that on your mind when you were running."

He shoved his hands through his hair and let out a heavy breath. For a moment he said nothing, and I knew it was best to let him have a minute to process it all. No doubt he'd worried and stewed the whole way home from the meet.

I knew I'd been forgiven when his hand reached for mine, the comforting warmth of his skin seeping into mine.

"I know, Layla," he whispered. "But, I keep thinking about it. Someone was in your car."

"Yes." No point sugar-coating it.

"And when I think what could've happened when your windshield clouded over with Vaseline." He squeezed my hand, locked his eyes with mine. "I'm glad Corey was driving."

"Me too."

"I mean, not that you couldn't have handled it," he amended. "I'm just glad you didn't have to."

"Thanks for your confidence, but I'm not so sure I could've handled it. I was shaken enough after the radio being messed with in my car."

"Kara must've been behind this too," he said.

"It's possible."

"I think I need to hear from you exactly what happened with her in the hallway the other day. And what happened in your car this afternoon."

"Can you stay for dinner?"

"Your parents cool with that?"

"I already asked."

"Let me call my mom," he replied. "I'm sure she'll be fine with it."

"Dinner," Mom called from the kitchen door, just as Luke finished his call to Gwen.

"Thanks for inviting me to stay, Mrs. Bradford," Luke said, pulling my chair back from the table and gesturing for me to have a seat.

Mom smiled as she watched me sit down, and I knew she'd noticed Luke's considerate act. And I wasn't unaffected myself. Despite the fact he'd already proven that chivalry wasn't dead, his sweetness never failed to surprise me.

We enjoyed Mom's baked spaghetti and garlic bread, letting the hearty Italian flavors rule our senses, not really in a hurry to get to the conversation we both knew was coming.

The uncluttered moments with family and good food were a refreshing change of pace.

And, of course, there was blueberry pie after dinner.

We helped clear the table and load the dishwasher, and Lucas impressed my mother once again with his domestic skills.

"Is it okay if Lucas and I use the office?" I asked Dad once the dishwasher was running. "He's been doing some genealogy research, and I'm helping him keep notes on it all."

The third bedroom in our three-bedroom house served as a home office, not just for Dad's business, but for all of us. I had a laptop I could use anywhere, but if I needed to plug up to the printer or spread out on a desk, the office was the place to work.

And since the office was somewhat private, it was really the only choice we had. Upstairs was only my bedroom and bathroom, and I wasn't going to ask about the two of us hiding out up there. But no way were we having this discussion at the kitchen table.

"Sure," Dad answered. "I'm not doing payroll until Monday."

"Thanks."

"That's very interesting, Lucas," Mom said. "Have you come across any surprises?"

"Actually, yes." Lucas seemed a hundred percent comfortable talking with my mom about this, although I knew for certain he'd leave out particular details. "Layla helped me at the courthouse yesterday, and we came across a name in a will that made some surprising connections for me.

"We compared what we found at the courthouse with my mom's records, and it seems we may be related to the Emerson's who own the antique store on Old Birch."

"Well, you keep us posted on how it's going."

"Sure thing, Mrs. Bradford."

And with that we made our way to the office. We took the two desk chairs and rolled them close together.

I told him everything about Kara's words to me in the hallway earlier in the week and today's events, starting with the picture on my lunch table up through the Vaseline on my windshield wipers. He listened without interrupting, just letting me tell the story from my point of view.

"I know Kara's involved in this," he said when I finished.

"Probably," I agreed.

"I've heard she's told people we're talking again. As in talking about reconciling. It's a lie, Layla. A total lie. We barely speak, other than I'm polite enough to say hello to her when we're in the same class."

"I know that," I assured him. "I didn't think twice about it when Miller said that this morning."

"Miller talked to you?" Lucas sat up straighter. "About Kara and me?"

"Well, kind of," I said. "He kind of warned me about her, and – "

I stopped there, stunned at the possibility. I hadn't thought about Miller again until this moment.

"What, Layla?"

"He... asked me out."

"Miller asked you out?" he whispered, but it was a furious whisper. If we'd been alone in the house he probably would've shouted. "After what he did to you the first day of school?"

His knuckles turned white and the muscles in his jaw tensed.

"Yeah. Well, first he apologized for that incident again. Then he said something about not being sure what the situation between you and me was. I asked him what difference it made to him, and that's when he said Kara could be pretty mean sometimes, and also he thought maybe if you and I weren't together I might consider going out with him. I turned him down, gently, of course."

"You should've slapped him."

The image of that made me laugh. Luke's expression told me he was serious and that made me laugh even harder.

"Can you really see me doing that?" I asked, pleased when he finally smiled. "And anyway, what if you're right about the evil people from our dreams being reincarnated? I didn't want to set Miller off."

"This is probably how it began for them," he said. "For the people we used to be. Little things, that didn't seem to matter much. Then it escalates into direct attacks, like what happened with your car. Or worse."

I didn't like the implications of that. I had a pretty good idea how it had ended for the two of us in our past lives, and if Luke was right, I shuddered to think what we might have to face.

But we had to deal with it.

"That's why I started this." I pulled my journal from my backpack and handed it to him.

He flipped through it, stopping every now and then to take a closer look at something. I said nothing, just let him look in silence, and I could tell he was as surprised as I'd been at the amount of information I'd recorded.

"This will be helpful," he said when he reached the end. "To keep track of everything that's happened."

"I thought so."

"But, you left something out." He turned back to the page that contained today's events. "The incident with Miller."

I took a blank sheet of paper from the back of the notebook, detailed my conversation with Miller, and stapled it to the already full page of stuff about the pictures, the loud music in my car, and the Vaseline on my wiper blades.

"Layla," Luke said, taking the now closed book from my hands. "This shouldn't leave your house. Unless you're coming to my house. I don't think you should carry it with you to school."

He was right. Not that I'd been thinking of sharing it with anyone else, but the implications of someone accidentally – or on purpose – reading my private stuff were huge. The average person would think I was either crazy or writing some sort of fictional novel. But if Lucas was right and we weren't the only ones reincarnated from the past, my journal falling into the wrong hands could be disastrous.

"I agree." I slid the journal back into my book bag. "It won't leave this house, except to go to your house."

"Let's forget about this for a while," he said, leaning toward me with a smile. "We have a date tomorrow night, and I want it to be special and normal. So no more talk about any of this. Not until after our night out."

I could do nothing but smile as he closed the distance between us and put his lips on mine, soft and sweet. Though his kiss was brief, he pressed his forehead to mine, and I closed my eyes, drinking in the feel of his skin and the warmth of his breath on my face.

My heart slid and skidded and rolled over in my chest, and I knew keeping my emotions safely locked inside was a losing battle. Luke had captured my heart, and whatever the consequences, there was no going back.

CHAPTER TWENTY-EIGHT

Of course, on the day of my date with Lucas, String City bustled with more activity than ever. A steady stream of people came in, and the phone rang off the hook.

Dad even called in Charlie, his assistant manager, who normally had Saturdays off.

The two of them handled the big things – instrument and equipment sales, guitar repairs, and so on. I manned the phones and took care of the smaller sales, like guitar strings, picks, and cables.

Constant guitar riffs and chords filled the store, both acoustic and electric, as customers tried out instruments and amps they wanted to purchase. I figured as far as part time work went, I had it better than most high school kids, because I got to listen to live music.

Every so often, Dad would look over at me and roll his eyes, all the while smiling like a big kid. He loved this business. Somehow, since coming here, he looked younger and the gray in his hair seemed less prominent.

My parents were so happy here, and I had to admit, I was too. My happiness existed despite the crazy circumstances I'd found myself in, and because I was in them with Luke. I wondered how my parents would react if they knew. Would their happiness be diminished?

I so didn't want that to happen.

So I'd do whatever I had to to make sure they didn't find out something supernatural was afoot in Sky Cove.

Because I loved them. Which made the fact I needed to press for information about my adoption most unpleasant.

***

The hectic business made the hours pass faster, which was a plus. Another plus was Dad letting me off thirty minutes early so I could have a little extra time to get ready.

I thought again how cool my parents could be.

I loved my brown cowl-necked sweater. It was the color of milk chocolate – anything chocolate was okay in my book – and soft and warm like a blanket. The way the neck draped across my collar bones made me feel elegant and grown up.

So it was no surprise I found myself reaching for the sweater as I got ready for my date.

I had no idea where we were going, other than Camden, but when I'd pressed Lucas for more information on the basis of needing to choose an outfit, he'd admitted that dressing up was not required.

So my dark blue jeans accompanied the sweater, the denim a dense navy and the bottoms cut to fit over the boots I'd worn to the first football game. My hair was down, both for looks and to keep the cold late-October wind off my neck, but thanks to a few minutes with a flat-iron, it was straight and sleek.

Small turquoise stones, set in silver, dangled from my ears, and as I put the finishing touches on my make-up, I was satisfied I looked pretty but not like I'd gone to a lot of trouble.

I wanted Luke to know I cared enough to look nice for him, but not to think I cared more about my appearance than things that really mattered.

Being a girl was a delicate balancing act.

As I made my way downstairs, I heard my mom in the office, probably checking her email and printing coupons.

I had a few minutes before Luke was due to arrive, so I decided now was as good a time as any to broach the subject of my adoption.

"Hey Mom," I said, poking my head in the office.

"Don't you look pretty?" She stood up from the desk and came across the room to hug me. "Lucas won't be able to take his eyes off you."

I smiled. Moms were really great for your self-esteem. At least mine was. Part of me hated to even bring up my adoption, because I didn't want to upset her. But another part of me knew she'd be cool with my questions.

"Mom I've been wanting to ask you something."

She tilted her head to the side and narrowed her eyes. Stepping out of the office, she made the few steps down the hall to the living room. I followed.

We sat next to each other on the brown leather couch, and by the way she was looking at me — all misty-eyed and melancholy — I got the feeling she thought I was going to ask something about boys or love.

Yeah, that was a road I wasn't going down with her. At least not yet.

"I've been wondering about my adoption." I said it softly, but to my ears the words sounded like a harsh blurt.

"You have?" Her expression changed completely, but despite it, she still seemed calm and steady. She reached to tuck a strand of light-brown hair behind here ear. "I wondered when you'd ask."

So she'd been expecting it.

"It never seemed important enough to ask about before."

"What's changed?" she asked.

I shrugged. It was a legitimate question and deserved a legitimate answer. I'd give her the most honest answer I could.

"Helping Luke with all his genealogy stuff just got me wondering, I guess." It was as close to the truth as I could get. "I know a lot about your family and Dad's family. And that's more than enough. It's not that anything's missing. I guess I just got curious about where my birth parents might've come from."

Mom reached for my hand, took it gently in hers. I hadn't realized I'd balled my fists until she smoothed out the tension with her touch.

"It's natural to wonder Layla," she said. "And your father and I have always told you that when you were ready, we'd tell you what we knew."

I didn't have it in me actually say the *words I want to know about it,* because the truth was I didn't really *want* to know. But I *needed* whatever information she had about my birth parents. Apparently, my silence was enough.

"We used a private attorney in Nashville," she began. "Your father knew of a couple through his work who'd adopted a child. They told us about the lawyer that had helped them, and when we came to the realization we weren't going to be able to have children the regular way, we contacted him.

"Your father handled most of the talking and phone-calling, but I gathered pretty quickly how it worked. There are attorneys all over the country who specialize in private adoptions and work closely with agencies. Sometimes a young mother chooses an adoptive family for her child. Other times a young woman who wants to allow her baby to be adopted comes to the attorney or an agency and asks for help in locating a family.

"The lawyer we worked with had contacts in various parts of the country. He put calls in to all of them that he had a family ready and willing to adopt. He warned us the waiting would be difficult, and he was right. But in only six months, we got the call that a young mother had chosen adoption for her unborn child."

"That was me?"

"It was you." Mom smiled. "Your father and I were open to the idea of an open adoption, which meant the birth mother would know where her baby was and the adoptive parents would allow her to be a part of the child's life at some point. But the young woman, your birth mother, didn't want that. I imagine giving up a child for adoption is difficult enough, and perhaps it was easier for her this way." Mom's melancholy smile told me that she truly felt for the young woman who'd given me up. It said a lot about my mom.

She went on. "Our attorney handled everything, and coordinated with the agency and with the young woman's attorney. We wanted her to have the best prenatal care possible, both for your sake and for hers, so we offered to pay for any medical expenses her insurance didn't cover."

"Were you able to be there when I was born?"

"No." Mom shook her head. "When she went into labor our attorney notified us and we flew to Boston immediately. But since it wasn't an open adoption and the birth mother didn't want to meet us or know who we were, we didn't go to the hospital to get you until after she'd left."

"Boston?" My pulsed kicked into high gear. "I was born in Boston?"

"Yes, at Massachusetts General, but the adoption was finalized in Tennessee, since that was the state we were residents of."

The realization that I was a New Englander by birth put a whole new spin on the notion that I might be somehow descended from the family of the woman in my dreams. I don't know what I'd expected to find out from my mother, but I hadn't prepared myself for this.

Hoping she couldn't see the stunned feeling written on my face, I squeezed her hand and smiled.

"Thanks for telling me," I whispered.

"I wish I knew more to tell you."

"No." I shook my head. "This is enough."

I heard Luke's car door open and close in the driveway. I stood up and smoothed my jeans over my thighs.

"You're lovely, sweetheart," Mom said. "Now go meet your prince."

I hugged her. Tight. And held on for longer than a moment. Whoever my birth mother was, she'd given me the greatest gift in the world by allowing this woman to be my mother.

"I love you, Mom."

The doorbell rang, and before I answered, I filed away this latest piece of information into my "tell Luke later" compartment. Because, after all, we weren't supposed to speak of our mystery until after our date.

CHAPTER TWENTY-NINE

Leave it to Lucas to plan the perfect date. He could've spent money on tickets to show at the Camden Civic Theater, which would've been fun, but wouldn't have allowed us the freedom to talk and laugh. He could've made reservations at an expensive restaurant where both of us would've felt out of place. But he didn't.

Instead, he found a family-owned diner that boasted traditional Tennessee barbecue. Who knew there would be barbecue in Maine?

Luke enjoyed the sweet and tangy shredded pork served on southern-style cornbread just as much as I did.

The little taste of Tennessee, and the opportunity to share it with him, warmed me from the inside, despite the cold temperature.

When we finished dinner, he drove toward the harbor. Even in the dark I could tell it was much larger than the one in Sky Cove. A string of restaurants and businesses seemed to be enjoying a booming Friday night. After an impressive job of parallel parking, he came around and opened my door, taking my hand as my feet hit the sidewalk.

"There's a store right up here I know you'll love," he said, squeezing my fingers.

The hand-painted sign above the door read *Aged Page,* and I smiled with excitement when I realized it was a used bookstore.

We found several volumes of Robert Burns poetry, each of us selecting a different one, as well as a collection of Tolstoy short stories which contained our latest literature assignment.

There was even a display of artsy jewelry, which looked to be handmade. I walked over to take a closer look.

"Is that sea glass?" I asked him, holding a pair of earrings with green-blue stones wrapped whimsically with silver wire.

"Sure is," he nodded. "Some people comb the beaches finding it and then make jewelry out of it."

"How cool." I hung the earrings back on the wrack, thinking maybe my mom would like a pair for Christmas.

The find of the evening though, was a DVD of "An Affair to Remember", which Luke grabbed immediately, saying we could watch it together back at his house.

The older lady who rang up our purchases smiled when she saw the movie.

"Nice to see the young folks enjoying films from my generation." She placed our items in a brown paper bag and handed it across the counter to Luke.

"It's a great movie," he replied. "We're going home to watch it right now."

"You two lovebirds look very happy." She turned toward me. "Reminds me of when my William and I were young and in love."

William? The name set off alarm bells in my head, but for a split second I couldn't figure out why. Then I noticed the elderly lady's nametag.

Patsy.

I looked up at Luke and could tell by his expression he'd seen it too.

Had we really run across Patsy Emerson by accident?

And were such occurrences accidents? Could I even believe in coincidence anymore?

"Are you Patsy Emerson?" Luke asked.

Her eyes lit up. Of *course* she was Patsy Emerson.

"Yes," she said, seeming pleased he somehow knew her. "Do I know you?"

"Not really," he answered. "My name is Lucas Ellis. And this Layla Bradford. We live in Sky Cove."

"My hometown. William and I lived there for many years."

"I know," Luke nodded. "I've been doing a bit of research into my family history, and discovered a possible connection to your family."

"Is that so?" Patsy asked, curious.

"Yes, ma'am. A woman named Amelia Cutler. I think she's the same woman in my mom's records, Amelia Cutler Light."

"I'm sure she is," Patsy said, her smile bright. "William had an aunt named Amelia Light, who was a sister to William's uncle Frank Cutler. Amelia and her husband moved out of the area, though, and William only met her once or twice as a small child."

Astounded was too mild a word for what I was feeling. I made a mental check to see that my chin wasn't on the floor and my eyes were still in their sockets.

Luke, meanwhile, continued on in his discussion with Patsy Emerson as if they were old friends and nothing more was at stake than his genealogy chart.

"Amazing that Layla and I would run into you here," he said. "Layla bought my birthday present at Emerson Antiques."

A nostalgic smile spread across the older woman's face. "William and I shared happy times in that house. Parkinson's disease hit him early, and we had to move to assisted living long before we thought we'd have to."

"If you don't mind me asking, how did you come to own the house?" Luke asked. "Layla and I have each been there several times and we think it's a really interesting place."

My heart beat so hard I thought surely Lucas and Patsy could hear it. Could we be about to discover the reality of who we once were? Could this chance meeting – if it even *was* by chance – really bring us closer to the truth?

"It came down to us from William's father, Walter. Before that it had belonged to William's grandfather, Arthur, who inherited it from his father George."

Which fit with what we'd learned at the courthouse about Arthur and George Emerson.

"Do you happen to know how George acquired the house?"

George Emerson was where we'd stopped looking. After seeing Amelia's name in the will, we'd headed home to look at Gwen's records.

"It seems I remember George inherited the house from his brother, though I'm not sure which one. According to what William told me, his great-grandfather – that would be George – had two brothers, Leo and John. I'm not sure which one of them was the original owner of the house."

Leo and John Emerson. Another fact to file away for later. Along with what I needed to tell Lucas about my adoption.

"I hope you have all this recorded somewhere. My mom started a notebook with names and places and stories her grandparents told her about." Luke reached for my hand, steadying me as if he knew how shaken I was by this latest bit of information. "It's where I first saw Amelia's name."

"My daughter has compiled some records. She keeps them on her computer, along with old family tales. There's one that tells of Leo becoming psychotic and some great tragedy befalling he and his wife."

Had Lucas not been holding my hand, I might've fallen over. "Some great tragedy" was likely just what we were looking for.

"What kind of tragedy?" Luke pulled me closer to him.

"I'm not sure really. But Leo and his young wife left Sky Cove never to be heard from again. George, William's great-grandfather, apparently forbade discussion of it. William said his father told him it was all malarkey that had been drummed up to make small town life seem more interesting."

"That could be," Lucas replied. "Small town life can get a bit redundant." He stepped toward the door, my hand still firmly in his. "Thank you for the information, Mrs. Emerson. I'll be sure to add it to my records."

We were almost to the door when Patsy stopped us.

"I just remembered," she began.

We turned back toward the counter.

"Amelia has a great-granddaughter. Brooke McKenna is her name. She was in Camden until just a few years ago, when she took a job in Boston."

"Really?" Luke looked down at me, then back and Mrs. Emerson. "Do you know where we could find her? If I could, I'd love to talk to her and find out what I can about Amelia and her descendants."

"She's a nurse. I believe she worked in the maternity ward at Penobscot Bay Medical. Now I hear she's down in Boston at Massachusetts General. Still helping deliver babies."

My knees knocked so hard I feared I couldn't walk, but as Lucas led me out of the store after thanking Mrs. Emerson one last time, somehow I found enough stability to put one foot in front of the other.

"Quite a coincidence, huh?" he said, as we made our way back toward his Bronco.

"More than you know." We reached the car, and rather than get in as soon as he opened my door, I turned toward him. "Luke, I have to tell you – "

He stopped me with a quick kiss on my lips. "Not now, Layla. Let's just save all this for tomorrow and enjoy the rest of tonight."

"But – "

Another kiss silenced me again. "I wanted this to be a normal night, just two regular kids on a date together. Not that I'm not glad we ran into Mrs. Emerson. It gives us more information and hopefully an idea where to look next. But we still have tonight, and I want it to be as normal as possible. We have a great movie to watch. Let's just head back to my house."

And just how could I argue with that?

"Okay." I smiled, feeling my heart latch onto him with an even firmer grasp.

CHAPTER THIRTY

The rain began before we made it back to Sky Cove. The thunder and lightening started sometime in the middle of the movie. Odd as a thunderstorm in October seemed, in the beginning it appeared to be nothing but a typical storm.

The rain was pelting down in sheets and the sky a constant flash by the time Nickie's voice came from the television saying "What makes life so difficult?"

"People," Terry replied. Luke's arm tightened around my shoulders, and I knew that Terry's words echoed what was swirling inside each of us.

Whatever difficulty had tortured the people we'd been, it was brought on by the actions of other people. Which was monumentally unfair. But I supposed that was just part of life.

"Rain keeps on like this, the water will be over White Bridge."

I sat up straighter, thinking about the fifteen-minute drive back to my house. Even if the water didn't rise over the bridge, there was still ponding and hydroplaning to consider.

"Don't worry about it," he added. "There's always a lot of water on this road when it rains like this. I'm used to it."

Yes, he would be, having lived here all his life. In Nashville, my experience driving in the rain mostly included traffic lights that had been knocked out due to lightning.

The storm raged on, more and more violent as the movie finished and we stood up from the sofa. Peering out the window, worry settled in my chest about the drive back to my house. There was so much water, and the wind howled and swirled with a vengeance.

I thought of myself as independent, but I was really glad Luke would be the one doing the driving.

He stepped up behind me, keys jingling in his hands, when a strike of lightening broke the sky and lit it up like it was the middle of the afternoon. The thunder that accompanied it was instant and deafening.

Gwen's bedroom door opened, her footsteps bringing her closer until she appeared in the living room.

"Can you believe this?" she said. "A thunderstorm this bad in October."

Somewhere in the house her cell phone rang. She disappeared down the hall, reemerging in the living room with the device pressed tight to her ear.

It was almost midnight, my curfew, so for anyone to be calling this late seemed odd. Something must be wrong.

"I see," she said. "And the road is impassable?"

I cut my eyes toward Luke and he shrugged.

Gwen ended the call and looked at us. "That was Mr. Geary who lives up the road, just past the bridge. White Bridge is flooded and one of the trees from his yard has fallen across the road."

"So we're stuck?" Luke asked.

"It seems so," she replied. "Even if there was another way back into town, I wouldn't want the two of you out in this. I'm just so thankful you weren't already out there driving. I'll call your mom, Layla."

Luke and I sat on the sofa as Gwen talked with my mother and assured her I was taken care of and that as soon as the road was cleared she or Lucas would drive me back home.

Before I knew it, pillows and blankets had been retrieved and an inviting bed had been made for me on the sofa.

Luke brought me a tee shirt and a pair of sweatpants that had to be his given how long the legs were. "They're probably way too big, but there's a drawstring."

"Thanks," I said, smiling. I liked the thought of sleeping in his clothes.

After changing in the downstairs bathroom, I made my way back to the living room, where I said a quick goodnight to Gwen and Luke. He kissed my cheek and winked before heading upstairs to his room.

Settling in under the covers on the couch, I replayed the events of the evening.

My talk with my mother and the discovery that I was born in Boston.

Running into Patsy Emerson in Camden and hearing the old family tale of a possibly psychotic Leo Emerson.

Discovering Amelia Cutler Light's great-granddaughter was a maternity nurse at a Boston Hospital.

The oddity of a thunderstorm in October and the road from Luke's house becoming impassable.

I wondered if the universe was aligning in an attempt to help us, or if opposing forces were conspiring to stand in our way.

Probably a little of both.

I decided sleep was a must, because in the morning there was sure to be a dissection of tonight's events. Plus, I still had to tell him what I'd learned about my adoption.

And from the looks of the books on the kitchen table, Gwen had been doing more reading.

I closed my eyes, forcing my mind away from the questions, and eventually, sleep came.

***

The beach was silent, save for the drizzling rain and light wind. It appeared a calm October rain, but I knew different.

I knew the brutality that had so recently filled this place. The rock outcropping stood tall and motionless, a mocking tribute to the violent act that had taken his life.

I knew I wasn't really here. In my mind I knew they'd already taken me from the beach where I'd fallen after they killed him. But somehow, I *was* here, and my consciousness was taking me to the opposite side of the rocks, where I'd never been before.

With startling clarity, even though I knew I was dreaming, I realized I was going to see what happened.

I was going to see him die.

The moment the flat ground beyond the outcropping came into view, my dream dropped into deafening silence. The waves that lapped at the shore were soundless. And though I still felt the cold rain and the chilly wind, the only thing that registered in my ears was stillness.

The branches they beat him with were huge, as big around as tree trunks it seemed. Over and over again they hit him, and with each blow I felt a corresponding jolt in my own body, a ripping and tearing through my heart. His face was bloody. His clothes torn. His body battered by their assault.

And when they were done, when he lay there lifeless and broken, they tossed his body into the tide, where it would soon wash away.

The leader of the mob turned toward me, but my eyes refused to focus. His features blurred to the point that he was hardly recognizable as a human being. I tried to move closer, but my dream held me immobile. The desire to discover the man responsible for the death of my beloved burned inside me like a furnace, and I cursed the dream that would not let me see him.

Anguish and misery washed over me, immense and powerful. The part of my mind that remembered I was sleeping on Lucas's couch and that he was safe upstairs in his own bed slipped further back in my awareness. I was lost in a sea of grief, the will to go on ebbing from my being with each breath.

And then I was not on the beach anymore, but rather inside a dark, damp shack. The floor was dirt. The walls some manner of stone that dripped with moisture from the humidity in the summer air.

Summer? When had it become summer?

Someone cried.

When had the sound returned to my dream?

She was alone. The woman who had my face and whose memories I had. Alone, writhing on an old wooden cot in the corner of the tiny room. She sobbed softly one moment, and moaned as if in pain the next.

My eyes narrowed, and my vision zoomed in on her face, the fear obvious and palpable. Whatever was happening to her was painful and frightening.

But worse than the pain and the fear was the loneliness. No one was there with her.

The smell of wet earth invaded my nostrils, coupled with the sweat from her skin. The light straining through the cracks between the stones in the wall was weak, as if the last vestiges of sunlight could not penetrate the darkness of the room.

Her dress hung halfway off one shoulder and a pitiful blanket draped her from the waist down. Her legs never stilled, with knees pulled toward her body, then laid flat on the cot.

The scream that ripped from her body seemed to reach inside me and shred my guts into minuscule pieces. The pain I felt for her... from her... was both emotional and physical. My abdomen burned and heaved and I wondered if either of us would survive this terrible ordeal.

Suddenly she was silent.

And the fire that had burned inside me cooled, the fear that had gripped my heart quieted.

Her face was blank, eyes opened wide, staring toward the ceiling. Frozen.

Blood poured on the floor beneath the cot in an increasing pool.

She was dead.

CHAPTER THIRTY-ONE

I bolted up from the sofa. My breath came in gasping gulps. I could not pull it into my body fast enough. Clammy sweat covered my forehead and my neck, and my pulse throbbed with frenzied speed in my temples.

My mind reeled, a tumult of feelings too raw and immediate to name. I tried to take note of my surroundings. The clock on the DVD player read 2:30 a.m. I reminded myself it had only been a dream, but the emotions coursing through me were so strong it was difficult to focus on reality.

Then he was there.

Lucas strode into the room with purpose, dropping to his knees on the floor in front of me. He took my face in his hands, forced my eyes to his.

"It was a dream." His eyes moved over my face, rapid and anxious. "It was a dream."

I knew he'd repeated it for his own sake, as well as mine.

"I saw it, Luke. I saw it all." My hands went to his face, gently touching him from forehead to cheeks to chin, reassuring myself he was alive. His skin was hot and flushed. "I saw him die. I saw her die. I saw both of us die."

Tears escaped my eyes and I dropped my head to his shoulder. He cradled me there, arms encircling me and running along my back.

"I know," he whispered. "I saw it too."

I burrowed my face against his neck, sliding my hands up the length of his back. My arms tightened around him, and his around me, as we tried to get close enough to each other to rid ourselves of the misery of our dream.

For a long moment we clung to each other there, in the dark of his living room, me on the sofa and him kneeling on the floor. And then I lifted my head and looked at him.

His mouth found mine, urgent and hot. He practically fused our lips together, as he climbed onto the couch with me. Careful not to make any noise, he leaned me back until I lay against the cushions.

One of his hands cradled my face, thumb stroking across my cheek. His other arm snaked around my waist, hand planted on the small of my back, pulling me closer still as he lowered his body on top of mine.

His mouth never left mine.

My arms went around him, inherent, as if they'd done it a thousand times before. The muscles in his shoulders rippled and bulged as he worked to keep the bulk of his weight off me.

Everything else in the world ceased to exist. The dream in which I'd watched him die faded, and I wanted nothing more than to be in this moment with him. Breath mingling, skin to skin, heartbeat to heartbeat.

I'd never been this close to a boy before. The few kisses I'd experienced before Lucas were clumsy and bland, the typical teenage attempt to be more grown up than we actually were. None of them actually showed affection.

Nothing close to *this*.

In my mind I knew I should feel nervous, tentative, but those feelings were nowhere to be found. I had no conscious memories from my past life of the two of us together in this way, but I supposed our souls must remember, because kissing Luke, holding him, being this close to him was easy and instinctive.

I was elated, and yet conflicted. I loved Lucas, of that I was certain. An expression of my love for him felt natural and perfect. A part of me wanted that so badly. But I knew going further would change things between us irrevocably. Going to the level of physical intimacy, no matter how right it felt, would somehow alter the course we were on. And our current course was difficult enough as it was.

And it was just too soon. Not to mention the doubts that still plagued me about the legitimacy of Luke's feelings for me. Teenage sex was an obstacle course fraught with dangers and baggage and was best left alone.

Luke slowed the kiss, but didn't pull away. All at once it changed from an urgent, blinding need to a sweet, tender show of love.

Surely it wouldn't hurt to enjoy it just a moment longer before I put the brakes on. Told him sex was just not in the equation at this point.

Part of me wondered how he'd react to that, even as he lifted his head to look at me, then pressed his lips to my forehead. I'd heard guys could be pretty upset when denied, especially when a girl seemed to be headed in that direction.

I hadn't meant to be a tease.

Abruptly, he pulled back and sat up.

"I'm sorry," he said.

"Huh?" I blinked a few times, pushing up on my elbows, cringing at my stellar response.

"We can't let things get out of hand." He shoved his hands through his hair and whispered, "Physically, I mean."

Of course he would be sensible. I shouldn't have worried. Although a tiny part of me would've liked it if he didn't want to stop.

Just like that, fear punched me in the stomach. What if that was it? What if he stopped because he didn't want to be with me that way? What if this was the first step in my ultimate rejection?

And why did I care when I knew very well sex was not something I was ready for?

Because I wanted him to want me, to love me, to feel for me what I felt for him. And the thought that maybe he didn't just killed me.

"We were just reacting to the dream," he said. "To how scared we were."

He might well have a point, but why couldn't it also be a reaction to what we felt for each other? The stupid, insecure girl inside me – who argued a guy like Luke could never really be interested in me – knew exactly why.

"It wasn't just about being scared," I said softly. At least it hadn't been for me.

"Considering the timing, what just exploded between us was more about the fear than our feelings for each other. A weird sort of assurance that neither one of us was dead, like what we saw in the dream."

I nodded. It made sense, the powerful need to get closer to each other, to hold on tight. We needed that affirmation of life I supposed.

The difference was, I needed it because I loved him.

"I'm really sorry, Layla," he repeated. "I shouldn't have handled you that way."

Unable to say what was on my mind – that I had been as much, or more, a participant as him – I just shook my head.

"Do you think you could stay down here?" I asked. "Just a little longer?"

And could I have sounded any more desperate?

I hated myself in that moment, but despite the fact that we'd reassured one another we were indeed, very much alive, I still wasn't quite ready to let him out of my sight.

His answer was to wedge himself against the back of the couch, lying on his side. He lifted his arms in invitation, and I cuddled next to him, my back against his front.

It felt warm and safe and right. And though my insecurities reared their ugly heads, there was no keeping myself from enjoying the feeling of his arms around me.

Even if I had to regret it later.

I was asleep in minutes.

***

This time the dream came peacefully.

We were in the back yard of Emerson House. Or rather, the people we'd once been were. They were older than us, but only slightly, as if they were young adults at the very beginning of their lives together.

It played out in my mind like scenes in a movie. I was aware that what I was seeing was not really happening, and I was free to watch or turn it off at my discretion.

She hung laundry on a line strung between trees. He pretended to help but really only tried to distract her. Hiding behind shirts and pants and blankets, he would peek out and try to startle her. I could tell it didn't work because all she did was giggle at him.

I was glad to see them happy, playful. Lucas and I had had too little of that. I imagined it was really the two of us... really Lucas and Layla... laughing and carefree.

He jumped out from behind a large blanket or towel and grabbed her by the waist. Though I knew it was a dream, I felt his arm around me, pulling my close to him.

At once I was no longer simply watching, but rather *in* the dream. I *was* her, with all her feelings and sensations. I looked through her eyes, felt with her heart. And what was inside her for this man was stronger than I'd ever imagined any feeling could be.

I was comforted by the assurance that being in the dream was my choice, and I could choose to stop at any time.

He kissed her. Well, it actually felt more like *Lucas* kissing *me*. I melted into him, letting him press me against him and wrap me in his arms. When the kiss ended and he looked at me, it was with wicked mischief. I chuckled at his expression, even as he grabbed my hand and began running toward the house.

Together we tumbled, laughing, through the back door of our home.

CHAPTER THIRTY-TWO

I woke from the dream the same way I'd gone into it. Peaceful and calm. The first threads of daylight spilled through the window of Lucas's living room, and his arm tightened around me.

Shifting around until I lay on my back, I looked up at him, and found his eyes already open and staring down at me.

The darkness was lifting outside, illuminating the living room a bit, and I found with the promise of daylight, my doubts were somewhat less.

I guess it's true about things always seeming worse in the middle of the night.

"That was a nice one," he whispered. "I think they were trying to make up for the last dream."

"Maybe so." I smiled up at him. "I think they wanted us to know their life wasn't always so awful. It was like they wanted to show us they had happy times too."

"I'm glad they did," he said. "I like thinking of them that way."

"Me too."

"We probably shouldn't be like this when my mom gets up." He pushed himself into a sitting position. "She wouldn't freak out or anything, but I don't want to give her any reason to think she shouldn't trust us."

"Are you going back upstairs?"

He cut his eyes toward the La-Z-Boy. "I think I'll hang out in the recliner. Mom won't think anything about that, especially once we tell her about the dream."

"Will you tell her about both dreams?" I asked, wondering how Luke would feel telling his mom about seeing the two of us happy and in love.

"We can keep the second one to ourselves." He winked and moved without noise to the recliner. "I think it was their gift to us."

"Okay." I snuggled down under the blanket again.

Luke pulled a crocheted afghan from the back of the sofa and settled into the chair. The small afghan barely stretched the long length of his legs, and didn't even come close to covering his chest. I supposed the Sky Cove Senior High tee shirt kept him warm enough.

"It's way early, Layla," he whispered. "May as well get a little more sleep."

I smiled, closed my eyes, and thought what a wonder it was that even after that terrible dream I could still feel giddy and happy.

With a smidgen of insecurity tossed in.

Uncertainty and reservation hovered in the back of my mind, but I shoved them away. I resolved to enjoy every moment with Luke, even if it meant heartbreak when our journey was over. If Luke's feelings for me ended once we solved the mystery of our pasts, so be it. I would have these memories to keep with me always.

***

Gwen's bedroom door creaked open and footsteps started down the hall. Not quite awake enough yet, I kept my eyes closed, thinking to myself if I just laid here a little longer I wouldn't have to re-live last night's death dream just yet.

I heard Luke's slight movements in the recliner next to me. I smiled, from the inside, my heart grinning and warmth spreading through me, at the thought that he'd stayed with me. He hadn't left me alone, even after we'd been comforted in the second dream.

I sensed the moment Gwen stepped into the room.

"Luke." Her voice was a whisper.

Luke shifted in the chair, and I heard the footrest descend softly.

"Morning," he said, his voice hushed, as if he didn't want to wake me. "I fell asleep down here."

"Another dream?" Gwen's intuitive streak was tremendous.

Luke must've nodded, because Gwen went on.

"A bad one?" she asked.

"Very." Luke's feet hit the floor with a quiet thud as he stood. "The worst one yet."

Why I continued to feign sleep I didn't know. Perhaps it had to do with my weird interest in hearing his exchange with his mother.

And from behind my eyelids, my doubts didn't seem so huge.

"I just didn't feel like I could leave her down here by herself afterward," he whispered. "Plus, I just kind of like being in the room with her."

Oh good grief. My heart turned over in my chest.

"We'll talk about it after breakfast," Gwen said. I could hear the smile in her voice. "Come help me get it started."

***

"I've been researching," Gwen said, as soon as I stepped into the kitchen.

She and Luke were making French toast and refused to let me help. Instead, I'd taken a quick shower, twisted my damp hair into a clip, and dressed again in the sweats Luke had loaned me.

I pulled the drawstring tight and rolled the waistband over four times to keep the bottoms from dragging the floor.

"I told her about the dream," Luke said. "And about meeting Patsy Emerson last night." He sat a bottle of syrup and a bowl of powdered sugar on the table and turned back to the cabinet to retrieve glasses. "What've you been researching?"

"About reincarnation." She motioned to a stack of books on the countertop across the room.

It was stacked with a dozen or so books. Scanning the spines, I read titles such as "The Other Me", "When Today Isn't Enough", and "Capture Your Past". I couldn't imagine where she'd come up with twelve books about reincarnation.

Luke must've had the same thought. "Bet you got some crazy looks at the library."

"I ordered them off the internet, silly," Gwen laughed.

Of course. You could find anything on the Internet.

And after the death dream, Lucas and I were willing to try most anything to uncover the truth and hopefully stop the frightening visions.

Luke pulled a chair out for me then retrieved a pitcher of juice from the fridge. He grabbed the platter stacked high with French toast just as Gwen turned off the stove and moved to the table. As soon as he dropped into the seat next to me, Gwen let loose with what she'd discovered.

"Theories on reincarnation are varied and widespread," she began, passing the food my direction. "But I've noticed some common threads among the different ideas. A lot of what's in these books is all the same thing, just with different syntax. Past-selves, reincarnate personas, mutual souls, that sort of thing."

Perhaps I'd been naïve for the last sixteen years, but it astounded me that so much had been written and so much thought had been put into theories of reincarnation. Of course, I'd never believed such a thing existed until a few weeks ago, so maybe I'd just been in the dark all my life.

"The overlap I found really interesting has to do with events that bring about reincarnation or spur resurgences of circumstances, such as what has happened to the two of you."

A resurgence of circumstances. What an interesting way to put it.

I passed the platter to Lucas, and once his plate was filled we both dug in.

Gwen was a great cook. Almost as good as my mom. The golden crispy toast combined with the sugary syrup did a great deal to sooth.

"Most reincarnation experts believe that there has to be an impetus for reincarnated souls to show themselves or to begin to act in ways similar to their past selves." Gwen took a book and opened it to a page she'd marked. "This book talks about intersecting events. These things can be anything really. Locations, objects, other people, and so on and so on. But this particular author believes there must be two intersecting events in order for people to begin to see or experience events from the past."

"How does that explain the fact that I was aware of my past life for years before this summer?" Luke asked.

"You were aware, but you knew nothing specific." Gwen pointed to a specific passage on the page and scooted the book across the table toward us. "This author would argue that at some point this summer, two intersecting events caused you to begin to see specifics, like Layla's face or actual events from their lives."

I touched Luke on the arm. "Like me coming here for the first time on July fourth."

"Exactly," Gwen said.

"But what's the second event?" Luke questioned.

"I think that's the million dollar question." Gwen leaned back in her chair and crossed her arms.

"It probably has something to do with how I'm related to the man in the visions," Luke suggested.

"The connections you and Layla have to the people in your visions may well be part of what brought all this to the surface," Gwen agreed. "Not all reincarnations are passed down through bloodlines. Some are random. But from what I've been reading, the ones that involve a blood connection are much stronger and much more intense."

Luke rubbed his temples. I reached back and put my hand on his neck, rubbing light circles on the muscles. Beneath the table, he put his hand on my knee and gave a gentle squeeze.

"Intense is an understatement." His words could not have been more true.

"I guess we're back to the courthouse, Layla."

Another trip to the courthouse might not be necessary, given what we'd learned from Patsy Emerson last night. And what I'd discovered during my conversation with my mom.

"I asked my parents about my adoption."

"You did?" Luke paused, fork halfway to his mouth.

"Did you learn anything that might be helpful?" Gwen asked.

"Maybe." I took a deep breath and turned toward Luke. "Last night Patsy Emerson told us that Amelia's great-granddaughter Brooke works in Boston as a childbirth nurse."

"Right." He narrowed his eyes.

"My mother told me yesterday that I was born in Boston."

***

My room felt familiar, yet lonely, as I sat on my bed later that night, flipping through the pages of the book I'd borrowed form Gwen.

Sometime after lunch the water level had receded enough that road crews could cross White Bridge and remove the tree that had fallen, and Luke had driven me home.

He'd seemed distant as he drove. I hated that. Hated feeling disconnected from him. My mind swam with possible reasons he'd want to distance himself from me, none of them good.

I decided to attribute it to the intensity of what we'd experienced. I figured talking about it anymore would've bordered on morbid.

I finished my homework before dinner, and after enjoying Mom's creamy beef and mushroom stroganoff and answering a bazillion questions about my date with Lucas, I'd gone to my room to read.

Just to make my reasoning seem more legitimate, I'd read fifteen or so pages of the Tolstoy story we'd been assigned in literature class.

And now the reincarnation book lay open in front of me.

First I scanned the pages Gwen had marked and the passages she'd highlighted. Most of the information outlined what she'd discussed with us over breakfast. With no idea what direction to go next, I began turning to random pages

A heading at the top of one chapter caught my eye.

The Gifting.

Propping myself with pillows against the headboard of my bed, I began to read.

It is not uncommon for those experiencing particularly strong or volatile reincarnation episodes to develop an ability that eventually proves useful. This phenomenon is referred to as The Gifting.

Research has documented such supernatural abilities as telekinesis, clairvoyance, mind-reading, and other physical abilities such as superior strength and speed. In most instances, The Gifting is temporary, and serves as a means to some end. If a reincarnated soul is in danger or having trouble achieving a necessary goal, The Gifting will provide the necessary skill to neutralize the danger or create success.

At first it sounded like mumbo-jumbo, but as I read it a second time it began to make sense. Danger or difficulty could be eliminated by "gifting" the reincarnate with some supernatural ability. Like mind-reading.

And then it clicked.

The words and phrases that had fallen into my mind. Not my own thoughts, but as if from the mind of another person. The person who was most likely targeting me, with the goal of destroying Lucas.

The person who was most likely the present-day version of the one who had led the mob to kill Lucas's past-self in the dream.

As realization dawned, the significance of the words I'd seen began to sink in.

I won't lose. Not this time.
No matter what I have to do.
It won't be long now, my love.
Even if I have to kill him.

Reaching for my backpack, I grabbed my notebook and began furiously recording the words that had bounced into my consciousness. I tried to describe everything about the situations. The way I felt alone and overwhelmed the first day of school. The happiness that bubbled inside me at The Pizza Place after the football game. The misery and anger that coursed through me that day in the cafeteria when I saw the pictures of Luke with Kara.

All three had been significant days, even before I picked up on the thoughts. That couldn't be an accident.

Putting words on paper as fast as they entered my mind, I hoped desperately that giving context to the episodes of random thoughts might give me some clue as to whose thoughts I'd heard.

CHAPTER THIRTY-THREE

The next several days came and went without dreams or visions. Nothing whatsoever was out of the ordinary, except that Lucas maintained a distance I could not explain. He didn't act different. We sat next to each other in literature. He walked me to my next class. He met me in the parking lot and walked with me to my car before heading off to cross country practice.

But something was off. Maybe he didn't look at me as often. Maybe he didn't walk quite as close.

He withheld himself from me, in a way I couldn't describe or put my finger on, but weighed on my heart nonetheless.

Our reactions to the last dreams could not have been more different. I wanted nothing more than to be closer to him after watching him die and seeing my own death. I supposed for Lucas, the opposite was true. He was pulling away.

As if I needed another reason to wonder if what he felt for me was real or just leftover from the past.

For lack of anything better to do in the afternoon hours – and to make myself think about *anything* but Luke and our dilemma – I finished reading the Tolstoy story. And when homework couldn't keep my mind off things, random playlists turned way up on my iPod helped drown it all out.

I was actually *happy* about the amount of chemistry homework Mr. Hartley assigned on Friday, and forced myself to think about that, rather than about Luke, as I walked in to Lit class.

"Leo Emerson was married to a woman named Lillian Bostridge," Luke whispered just as Mrs. Chadwick stood up to start literature class.

Way to drop a bomb. He'd been back to the courthouse, I assumed. Or at least done some research that lead him to Leo and his wife.

And he'd done it alone. Without me. And waited until I couldn't respond before telling me.

Suffering through the class discussion on *Ivan Ilyich* was torture. I had so many questions and no way to ask them. Part of me wanted to be angry that he'd excluded me, but the bigger part of me felt I had no right to expect to be included in his family research.

Except that it might well affect me just as much as it affected him.

I glanced over at him toward the end of Mrs. Chadwick's lecture and noticed his hand clenching into a fist over and over again. Clearly he was as agitated as I was.

Good.

I wasn't exactly mad at him. Frustrated was a better word.

And yes, my feelings were hurt. But I wouldn't let him see that. I shoved it all inside, locking my disappointment away and refusing to let it show on my face. When the bell rang to end class, I put on a neutral expression and left the room.

As we walked toward my U.S. History class, he filled me in a bit more.

"Thanks to Patsy, I knew what to look for," he explained. "Once I had the name Leo Emerson, it wasn't hard to find his name and the name of his wife."

"And what did you discover about them?"

"They owned the house in the mid 1800s. There's no record of children, and no date of death listed. When the house was abandoned, it went to his brother. Which was how it eventually ended up being William and Patsy's."

"So, are we now operating under the assumption that one of my birth parents was somehow related to Lillian Bostridge?"

"I think that's what we've got to assume at this point." We stopped just short of my classroom door, leaned against the wall out of the way of the traffic. "We know I'm connected to the Emerson's. The logical partner to that is that you're connected to Lillian's family. Even if you never find out who your birth parents are, I figure it's a safe bet one of them is descended the Bostridges. And you coming here to Sky Cove must be one of the two intersecting events that caused the reincarnation visions to really amp up."

I nodded. It made sense, as much as anything in this whole mess could make sense. "And we still have no idea what the second event could be."

Luke shook his head. "Maybe we should talk to Brooke McKenna. We know she's connected to the Emersons, that she has some kind of knowledge of the tragic story that happened to Leo and Lillian."

"And she works in Boston. As a labor delivery nurse." I lowered my voice as two cheerleaders, Jade and Kristin, walked into the room. Though they'd actually been okay and given me no indication of taking part in Kara's bad attitude, I wasn't willing to risk them overhearing me.

"But she didn't work there when you were born." Luke shifted closer to me. "Patsy said she worked somewhere else until just a few years ago."

"It can't be coincidence, Luke. Her job. The fact that she's in Boston. It's too much overlap to be insignificant."

"You're right." He looked at his cell, checking the time, and I knew he was going to have to head to his next class. "Can you come to the house this afternoon?"

I nodded.

"I'll call you when I'm done with practice and swing by and pick you up. You can have dinner with Mom and me and we'll figure out where we go from here. I have a few more theories we ought to talk about."

"So do I," I said. "But you don't have to pick me up. I can drive out, so you don't have to drive back into town to take me home."

He shook his head. "Don't want you out by yourself at night. Not with all this going on."

I started to protest, but he stopped me with a pleading look. "Let me do what I can to protect you."

And how could I argue with that?

Just like that, my emotions were fully engaged again, and the pendulum that was my doubt about Luke's feelings swung back to the side of believing they were genuine and real.

If it was a delusion, I was buying it willingly.

And probably regret it later.

***

I called Adrienne that afternoon. I'd been woefully neglect in keeping in touch with my best friend in Nashville. Part of me felt guilty for making new friends in Sky Cove, but I supposed that was the natural way of things. And I was thankful for Jessie and Marsha and the other girls I'd met. It was good to be able to share the day-to-day happenings with them.

But the prospect of hearing Adrienne's voice somehow made the vortex of my crazy emotions seem less daunting.

"Layla!" she squealed when she answered the call. "I miss you!"

"Me too. How are things?"

"Same as usual," she said. "High school drama and all that goes with it."

I thought of Kara and the pictures on the lunch table. "Some things are the same wherever you are."

"Uh oh. What's doing with the boy you told me about?"

I wanted so badly to confide in her, but how could I possibly tell her what was going on without sounding like a total freak?

"It's just weird," I began, deciding to just skim the surface. "We're still together, I guess, but there are some things from the past that just keep creeping up and making me wonder."

"An ex-girlfriend," Adrienne declared. "They so suck."

I laughed. It was true. Ex-girlfriends sucked.

"Sort of," I replied. "Anyway, I just keep having these doubts, like maybe he doesn't really like me as much as he thinks he does. Like any minute now the new will wear off and everything's going to just fall apart."

True enough, even though Luke's ex-girlfriend was only a small part of the problem.

"Layla, you've always had a self-confidence issue."

Really? I had? I mean, I'd always known I wasn't cut out for "popular status", but I'd also felt right at home in the middle of the pack. I was comfortable.

"What makes you say that?" I asked, even as my doubts about Luke waved red flags in my face.

"Oh, I know you don't think you have any issues with your self-image, and in a lot of ways you don't. You're smart and you embrace that. You're happy being who you are, and you don't kill yourself trying to fit in with the popular crowds. All of that's good. But I don't think you've ever looked at yourself and thought of yourself as pretty or attractive. I think when it comes to guys, you've always just sort of wondered what they could possibly see in you."

She was right, I realized. She was absolutely right. Adrienne was pretty and thin and stylish, and I'd always just thought of myself as plain, inside and out. Hadn't I been surprised by Luke's interest in me?

"Does your silence mean you think I'm right?" Adrienne asked.

"I see your point," I said. "I guess it's because I never wanted it to matter what a guy thought of me."

Far less likely to get hurt that way.

"But what Lucas thinks matters, doesn't it?" she asked.

Did it ever. "Yes, it does. Very much."

"Then trust him. If it falls apart, it falls apart. You won't be the first person to experience that. But if you keep doubting, you might miss out on something great."

"I need your pep talks more often," I said with a smile.

"Yeah, yeah, I'm a regular teen shrink."

"You should come visit, maybe spend some of the summer here with me."

"Maybe I will."

When I hung up, I felt somewhat better. At the very least, I had a better understanding of where some of my doubts came from.

Now if I could just have a better understanding about what craziness went on in the past and what Lucas and I were supposed to do about it in the present.

CHAPTER THIRTY-FOUR

Gwen wasn't home when Luke and I arrived. A note on the kitchen table said she'd gone to the dentist and would be back in time for dinner.

Luke headed upstairs to drop his backpack in his room and I followed. I pushed the door wide open as I stepped in, watching him stand at the window for a long moment.

"Layla, I need to apologize again about the other night," he said, when he finally spoke.

I said nothing, my silence prompting him to turn and look at me.

"For the way things got out of hand between us."

I didn't know what to say. I wasn't sorry about it, especially since we'd both had the good sense to put the brakes on. And feeling the way I felt about him I didn't have it in me to regret the way we'd clung to each other after the death dream.

It bothered me that he was sorry.

"I mean, I'm not sorry I kissed you like that," he corrected. "I'm just sorry I pushed you that far."

Okay. So maybe he wasn't sorry about the kissing. Maybe it wasn't dislike or regret. Maybe he felt...

"I feel guilty for manhandling you, and I wish you'd say something because I'm so incredibly sorry."

"Don't apologize." I stepped closer, though a good five feet remained between us. "You have nothing to be sorry for. You didn't do anything. It was a reaction to what we saw in the dream. It was natural. And it was *mutual*."

"It's just... I don't know." He shoved his hands through his hair and walked back toward the window. He took a deep breath, shoulders slumping and turned to look at me. "We're in the middle of this insane situation, and I feel like I have to hold myself back and not feel what I'm feeling so we don't cloud over things or piss off the bad guys, so we can keep our focus."

Where was he going with all this?

"And I want you to know that I do think of you that way." He walked closer, angled his head. "I mean, in *that* way."

My heart went wild, and I wondered if he could hear it. The look on his face melted everything inside me, turning my brain to mush.

But he wasn't finished.

"Sometimes I look at you and I forget all about strange dreams and visions and past lives, and all I can think about is how pretty you look and how lucky I am and how proud I am that you want to be with me. Sometimes all I want is to be a normal eighteen year-old guy who's crazy about his girlfriend."

Ohmigosh. Wow.

And yet, at the same time my heart soared with elation, I wondered if he *could* be that normal eighteen year-old. I wondered if he *could* feel about me the way a guy felt about his girlfriend under regular circumstances.

But for however long he *wanted* to, I'd oblige.

"Do you think," he began, moving to stand right in front of me, "that for a few minutes, we can just be Luke and Layla, happy to be together?"

I nodded, knowing that I'd take any opportunity to make a memory with him. If the time came that memories were all I had, I aimed to have plenty.

With hands so gentle and so soft, he framed my face, tracing his thumbs beneath my eyes with a kind reverence that stole my breath.

I was undone.

His lips lowered to mine and my eyes fluttered shut, just like I'd seen in the movies. A delicious swirling commenced in my stomach as I felt the press of his mouth. Somehow my arms wound their way around his neck, though I could not recall giving them the order. One of his hands slid to the small of my back and pulled my body flush against his.

For several long moments we stood like that, in the middle of his room, lost in the kind of kisses I'd thought only happened in fantasies. Time seemed suspended, as if what had been and what was yet to come didn't exist. There was no hurry, no urgency, no pressure for more than this. Just us, Luke and Layla, two kids who'd managed to find happiness in the midst of teen angst and drama.

And for those moments, I could almost put my doubts aside. Almost.

Gwen's key in the front door broke the spell, but not before Luke pressed his forehead to mine and smiled.

All I could do was smile back, so lost in love I would gladly drown.

***

We settled once again at the kitchen table. It still amazed me that Luke, Gwen, and I could discuss the reincarnation issues over dinner without fear of indigestion or choking. It now seemed as normal as anything else, and I couldn't decide whether that was good or bad.

"So something weird happened at practice today," Luke said.

I paused and looked over at him.

"We were running the trail down through the neighborhood where Emerson house is. I was running the old road that winds with the creek, and it was like all of a sudden I could've run as fast as I wanted to."

"You've always run fast, Luke," Gwen said.

"But I mean, I had to hold back. I was giving the run a hundred percent already, but all of a sudden I had more inside me, like I could've taken off and gone faster than a human should be able to. I had to force myself to run normal."

"Has that ever happened before?" I asked.

"Once last week, but I just thought it was my mind playing tricks on me. But today..." He let his voice trail off.

"It's *The Gifting*," I said, grabbing the book from the edge of the table and flipping it open to the pages I'd marked.

Gwen took the book and read the passage out loud. Luke just stared, wide-eyed, like he couldn't believe it.

"So, you think I've been gifted with a supernatural ability?"

"It's not so hard to believe," I said. "We're already experiencing visions and dreams about some past tragedy. Why shouldn't we get to have super-powers too?"

Luke smiled. "Guess you're right."

"Besides, I think I've discovered what my gift is."

CHAPTER THIRTY-FIVE

"You're reading the mind of the bad guy?" Luke's words sounded half question, half exclamation.

"Not really mind-reading," I said. "It's more like random thoughts just drop into my consciousness."

"Either way, it's a tremendous insight," Gwen put in.

"And now we've pretty much got confirmation that this person is after you, and wants me out of the way." Luke cleared the plates from the table and loaded them into the dishwasher.

"I think we have to assume this somehow parallels what you've seen in the dreams and visions," Gwen said. "That whatever befell these two people was the result of someone's intense jealousy."

Luke leaned against the counter and shoved his hands through his hair, letting out a huge, frustrated sigh. "Should we expect to be abducted and murdered, too?"

My breath caught in my throat with a sharp pain that radiated into my chest. Was it possible?

"I don't want to even think that," Gwen said, pulling me to her side with one arm and grabbing Luke's hand with the other. "The pranks you've experienced so far have been rather juvenile, even though the tampering with Layla's car could've been dangerous. Perhaps if the villain of this scenario has been reincarnated in a teenager, his vengeance will also assume adolescent form."

"We've thought all along that Kara was behind the stunts," Luke said.

Gwen nodded. "She'd be a likely suspect, if the thoughts Layla's been reading didn't indicate a male."

"It's possible Kara's being used," I suggested, looking at Lucas. "Everyone at school knows your history with her, and everyone is aware of her jealousy. She'd be an easy tool for our culprit."

"Miller's behavior makes him suspect," Luke said. "And the fact that Lance also asked you out creates suspicion. He always turns things into a competition, like he's got to be better than me all the time. Both of them run in the same circles as Kara."

"Which would make it easier to get her on board with the plan."

The phone rang, and Gwen went down the hall to her office to answer it. By the sound of her voice it must've been someone she was glad to hear from.

With her chatting happily down the hall, Lucas turned to me.

"I have another theory," he said once Gwen was gone. "About something we saw in the dream the night of the storm."

My muscles tightened as I remembered what we'd seen that night. "What is it?"

"I think Lillian died in childbirth."

All the breath left my lungs and my chest burned. At first my mind resisted the idea. The grief was too great. But after a moment I saw the logic, as images from the dream floated across my mind.

"She was alone when we saw her," Luke said. "Like she was hiding. If she realized she was pregnant, it makes sense that she'd try to get away from whoever had taken her. She was by herself in that abandoned shack. It didn't hit me right off the bat, but when I thought about it later," he stopped, took a deep breath. "The way she was moving, the sounds she was making, it made me wonder."

He paused again. I still said nothing, too dumbfounded to put words together.

"I don't know much about childbirth, obviously," he said, then swallowed hard. "But the blood on the floor underneath her..." his voice trailed off.

"I know," I whispered, finally finding my voice. "I think you're right."

"I googled some things about childbirth complications," he went on. "There are a number of things that can happen that would cause a woman to hemorrhage like that, especially if she hasn't had proper prenatal care."

"I don't even know how to feel about this," I said. "I mean, it's awful. The most terrible thing I can imagine. But since I've obviously never been pregnant, I don't have any sort of frame of reference for this kind of loss."

"Me either." He came over and kissed my cheek. "I wonder if by reincarnating into younger versions of themselves, they might have been trying to make it easier on us. Not that we don't have a lot at stake, but at least there's not a pregnancy to worry about."

I thought back to the night of the dream, when physical closeness exploded between us. Keeping our heads level in the midst of a hormone overload suddenly took on more meaning.

The thought of suffering that kind of loss devastated me, even though I had no knowledge of it. I grieved for Lillian, for what she must've endured in that shack all alone.

For the first time since the dreams began, I knew what I had to do. It was time to not just endure what she showed me. It was time to embrace it. Embrace her.

Embrace *them*.

"We've got to ask them again, Luke," I whispered. "We have to ask them to show us what happened."

CHAPTER THIRTY-SIX

Driving through town on our way to my house, we noticed The Pizza Place was packed with cars. Luke pulled his Bronco into the parking lot.

Luke looked over at me and smiled. I shrugged. Why not.

"Might as well go in and say hi," he said, shutting off the ignition. "We deserve a bit of fun before we try to have a conversation with our past selves."

His caramel-smooth voice held a hint of levity as he said *past selves*. I liked that. No sense in being über-serious about it every single moment.

The inside of the restaurant revealed all the major players from Sky Cove Senior High. Apparently the lack of a home football game tonight hadn't kept kids away from the weekly gathering at The Pizza Place.

Luke's cross country buddies, Corey and Will, sat in the far corner of the dining room with a couple of other runners and, to my surprise, Marsha and Jessie. I smiled at the possibility of a potential romance. I'd seen Jessie eyeing Will, and Corey had been flirting inconspicuously with Marsha. The perpetual texters from Lit class huddled together over their cell phones at another table. A group of cheerleaders,

Kara included, glared at us with disapproval from their booth, and in the center of the room, where they could attract the most attention, sat Lance, Miller, and a few other "upper crust" boys. Someone at the center table held a cell phone, blasting a ring tone that was the same death-metal, headache inducing music that blared from my radio the day someone messed with my car. I made a mental note.

Kara's stare didn't let up, and Lance popped up from his seat and walked toward us.

"Maybe this wasn't such a great idea," Luke said.

I almost agreed, until I saw Marsha and Jessie waving at us while Corey and Will grabbed two empty chairs.

I needed to be able to stand my ground, even if it was only in my own mind, and rise above the pettiness.

"Don't worry about them," I answered.

"Hey guys." Lance turned on the swagger as he reached us.

"Hi Lance," I said. Luke just nodded.

"Can I buy you a Coke, Layla?" Lance asked.

Good grief. How big of a moron was this guy? Rumors were flying at school that Luke and I were an item, and though we hadn't confirmed it, I'd just walked into the restaurant with him. And Lance was hitting on me. In front of Luke. Geez.

Part of me wondered if it was some weird, convoluted way of making fun of me. A kind of get-the-new-girl-interested-then-drop-her-like-a-piece-of-trash ploy.

Whatever. Either way, he was wasting his time.

"Lance," Luke began, much calmer than I would've expected. "I know I haven't been exactly clear about this at school, and that's my fault. But I'm fixing it right now." He slipped his arm around my waist and pulled me flush against his side. "She's with me." He shot his eyes toward Kara, who'd yet to break her stare. "And vice versa."

Lance's eyes narrowed, and he nodded in what appeared to be acceptance. Luke took my hand as we walked toward the table with our friends.

"Risky," I whispered, "if what we believe about the villain is true." Though honestly, I didn't care. My heart was giddy.

Luke just smiled. "Maybe I don't care. I'm tired of pretending. If whoever he is wants me out of the way, then bring it." He squeezed my hand and brushed a soft kiss across my cheek. "I'm not going anywhere."

CHAPTER THIRTY-SEVEN

Silence filled the house at midnight and seemed almost deafening in the darkness. My parents had finally fallen asleep, and the neighborhood traffic had slowed to almost nothing. Earlier, I scrolled through the library of music on my iPod, searching for something appropriate, but finally decided the silence was better.

I pulled my chair over to the window, and sat facing the direction of Emerson House. Though I couldn't see it, I imagined that looking toward it would connect me to them. Closing my eyes, I called to mind the faces of the man and woman from my dreams. My face. Luke's face. Lillian and Leo. The scenes played in my mind, and I let the images come. Even the frightening ones. They were all pieces to a puzzle that Luke and I had to solve.

Questions formed in my mind, faster than I could process them. There was so much we needed to know.

"Please show us what we need to know," I whispered in the darkness. "Help us find the truth."

***

It was like a picture album. Images. Still-shots. Flipping through my consciousness one at a time. The two of us smiling, laughing. Together in our home. Simple, everyday things, like cooking, talking. Faces of others who were a part of my life. Unfamiliar, yet not unpleasant.

After a moment, I realized it was chronological. The picture album that was playing in my dream actually told the story of their life together.

I smiled at the picture of the two of us running toward the creek behind the house, holding hands, playful smiles wide on our faces. The next pictures flashed by so quickly my mind barely had time to register them.

A body, still and lifeless on the creek bank. Long blond hair matted with blood. The remains of her dress ripped and torn, revealing flesh peppered with bloody cuts. The two of us, shocked. Leo, kneeling, looking for signs of life. The eyes of the dead woman staring, cold and blank. The face familiar.

Kara Jennings.

***

My phone buzzed at 5:45 a.m. As I pushed the button to answer, I unfolded myself from the rocking chair where I'd fallen asleep.

"Lucas," I answered, reaching up to rub the stiff neck I knew would accompany me all day.

"You okay?"

"Yes," I answered. "You?"

"Stunned."

I took a deep breath, willed myself awake. "We knew she had to be behind the pictures at school. I guess it's not such a stretch to think that she's somehow connected to all this."

Luke blew out a breath, frustrated. "We asked them to tell us the truth, and instead we get more questions."

"We have another piece of the puzzle." In truth, I was as frustrated as Luke, but I knew we had to figure out what this meant. "If we follow the idea that what's going on with us now parallels what happened in the past, then the woman in the dream must've been a former girlfriend of his."

"Just like Kara's my ex." I could hear the wheels turning in Luke's mind. "Then you moved to town and caught my eye, and squashed any chance she might've thought existed that the two of us would get back together."

I smiled. I'd *caught his eye*. I was also pretty fond of the term *squashed*. He had such a way with words.

"We've wondered if maybe Kara is being manipulated into causing us problems," I said. "It's possible that her jealousy was used in the past as well, as a way to try and come between the two of them."

"If so, it didn't work out too well for her."

Understatement.

"So here's what we think we know so far." I grabbed my notebook and a pen out of my backpack and began jotting things down. "These two people were married, and someone wanted him out of the way. This fits with what were told the last time we asked them to give us information, and also with the thoughts I've been picking up. After what we just saw, we have to assume that the ex-girlfriend was used to try and come between them."

"And when that didn't work, he killed her?" Luke questioned.

"That's my best guess. Because she knew who he was and what he was capable of. I sure hope your mom is right and whatever wrong deeds our present-day bad guy does fall under the category of teenage pranks."

"I'm going to try to find Brooke McKenna today. It's about a three and half-hour drive to Boston. Maybe she can help us fill in some of the blanks. Do you think your parents would let you go with Mom and me next Saturday?"

"Maybe."

"Well, don't say anything just yet. Wait and see if I'm able to locate her. If I do, I'll call and talk to your mom myself."

"Okay." A smile spread across my face. Such a gentleman.

"There's a home football game next Friday night," he said. "Will you be my date this time?" Amusement was evident in his voice.

"I was the fist time, you know," I answered, laughing softly.

"Yeah, but I meant officially. Since I went public in a major way at The Pizza Place last night."

"Officially," I agreed.

CHAPTER THIRTY-EIGHT

I thought about Lillian all week long. Not that she and Leo hadn't been on my mind a lot before, but after Luke's suggestion that Lillian had died in childbirth, thoughts of her never left me.

The scene in the dream where we'd watched her die played over and over in my mind. As did the happier moments we'd witnessed between the two of them.

I found myself constantly wondering what it must've been like for her, to have been abducted by a mad man, only to realize she was carrying the child of her beloved husband who'd been murdered by the very man holding her captive.

Though I had no real idea the feelings of protectiveness an expectant mother experiences, there were times when the sheer panic Lillian surely felt crept up inside me.

It made me angry.

Which was why, on Thursday morning, I came to school with a scowl on my face.

I shouldered my way through the crowd in the lobby, not in the mood for anybody's chit chat, hoping to make it to the chemistry room without having to make nice with anyone. Of course, as soon as I stepped out of the mass of people and into the hallway, I saw Kara Jennings and her two cronies, Erika and Tina, huddled around something or someone near my locker.

What were they doing in this hallway?

Good grief, what if it was another sign on my locker?

A few more steps and I realized just what they were up to.

"I heard you're the one who painted the banner for tomorrow's football game." Kara's voice dripped with snottiness.

She was speaking to Phoebe.

And I assumed she was referring to the huge banner than hung above the front doors of the school, depicting a football player running down the field as the crowd and cheerleaders urged him on. It was a really good painting, and though I hadn't stopped to inspect, it looked like each player's name was listed across the top.

I'd heard Phoebe had a talent for art.

I hung back, not wanting to make my presence known just yet, hoping to figure out why Kara had a beef with Phoebe's artwork.

"I had help," Phoebe answered, not seeming too bothered by Kara's attitude.

"But you were the one in charge," Tina snapped. "We heard it from the others in the art class."

Phoebe just shrugged. "So?"

"So, you made the cheerleader on the far left of the front row fat." Kara spat the last word out like poison. "And everyone knows that's where I stand."

Ah, so that was it. Kara's ego had been damaged. Well boo hoo.

"Maybe I didn't paint that one," Phoebe offered, grabbing a textbook and two notebooks from her locker.

"No one else would dare make fun of Kara that way," Erika said.

I fought the urge to laugh out loud.

"You mean everyone else is afraid of her." Phoebe looked straight at Kara. "Don't expect me to apologize for the fact that I'm not."

"I'm going to the principal about this." Kara stomped her foot. She actually stomped her foot like a child throwing a temper tantrum.

"Go ahead," Phoebe said. "You can't prove anything intentional was done. And besides that, no one's going to pay any attention to that little figure on the banner. Despite what you seem to think, you aren't the center of everybody's universe."

Well, thank you Phoebe whatever-your-last-name-is, for saying what I've been thinking ever since school started.

The threesome of cheerleaders turned to head back toward the front office, and Kara caught sight of me.

She glared at me, like I was a bug she was about to smash, and for the first time, I felt nothing. Her disapproval didn't make me feel small or insignificant.

It was almost like her opinion meant nothing.

Wow. How nice.

"I'm sure you just love this," she snarled as she walked by.

I just smiled, eyebrows raised. In truth, I hadn't noticed the fat cheerleader on the banner. But I wasn't going to let her know that.

As they breezed past, Tina's shoulder just happened to brush mine, shoving me into the wall.

And the only thing that bubbled inside me was laughter.

Not humiliation. Not the desire to suddenly become invisible.

Instead, all I could do was laugh.

And look at Phoebe and say, "Nice job."

***

Noisy fans made it difficult to talk at the football game Friday night, but I figured that was part of the charm. Bundled in a turtleneck and a sweater, as well as a winter coat, I snuggled close to Luke and felt his arm come around me.

Marsha, Jessie, and Tiffany sat to my right, and to Luke's left were Corey and Will. We'd formed our own little tribe, it seemed, and everyone seemed happy and at home.

After the first touchdown of the game, the loud cheering gave Marsha the perfect opportunity to ask about my status with Luke.

"So, it's official now?" She wiggled her eyebrows in that playful way that I'd become accustomed to. "You and Luke?"

I grinned until I thought my cheeks might split. "Yeah. Official."

She elbowed me and giggled. "It's about darn time!"

We laughed and cheered Sky Cove Senior High to victory, and when the time came to head to The Pizza Place Jessie and Will climbed into Luke's Bronco to ride with us, while Marsha and Tiffany piled into Corey's truck.

As expected, The Pizza Place was crawling with people, exactly the way it always was after a home game, except that unlike last time, the cold wind forced everyone inside. Spotting an available table in the back, the seven of us pushed through the crowd.

Halfway there, words started dropping into my mind. Grabbing Luke's hand, I stopped where I stood. He motioned for the others to go on. I ordered myself to breathe, then closed my eyes and let the thoughts form.

In the darkness behind my eyelids the words began to fall into place.

You belong to me.

The words reached my consciousness with such malice that I swayed on my feet, Luke's arm around my waist steadying me.

"He's here, Luke," I said. "I figured he had to be close the other times I picked up on his thoughts, but this time..."

"What was it?"

"The words were 'You belong to me'." I raised my eyes to Lucas's. "But I could feel the venom in his thoughts. He's through waiting. And he's in this room right now."

Luke's eyes darted around the room, scanning. Trying to figure out who it was would be like searching the beach for a specific grain of sand. Practically everyone was here.

"Let's just act normal. We can't risk having him figure out you've been reading his thoughts." Taking my hand again, he led me over to the table.

"Headache," he explained as we sat down. "Let's get our drinks ordered so Layla can take some medicine."

I spent the rest of the evening both hoping to pick up another thought and praying I wouldn't so I could enjoy the company of Luke and our friends. In the end, I decided to be grateful that nothing else invaded my mind.

And I managed to love every minute of my first official public outing as Luke's girlfriend.

CHAPTER THIRTY-NINE

We left for Boston before dawn on Saturday morning. My parents had agreed to let me go with Gwen and Luke, and I felt better knowing we hadn't had to be completely untruthful about our reasons.

Other than seeing Brooke, the main reason for our trip was for Luke to see the course for the Boston Athletic Association 5K, which he planned to run in April, on the same day as the Boston Marathon. He'd been planning the run since the spring, before I'd moved to town and the reincarnation insanity had begun.

Gwen had also promised to take us to a couple of other cool spots, like the Old North Church, and the bar from the old TV show "Cheers".

Thanks to the late night at The Pizza Place, Luke and I dosed most of the way to Boston, while Gwen drove.

Even though I'd grown up in a large city, Boston was different. Maybe it was because I understood and appreciated the historical significance of the city, or maybe because of the mix of modern architecture and historic looking buildings, but I felt like I'd gone back in time.

Like everything else I'd experienced since moving to New England, it felt new and familiar all at the same time.

I refused to believe that it had anything to do with the fact I'd been born in this city.

The next stop was lunch. The *Bull and Finch Pub* at Beacon Hill had been used for the exterior shots of the "Cheers" bar. I'd seen reruns of the show, and as Luke, Gwen and I walked toward the building, I half expected a Sam Malone and Diane Chambers to appear.

The inside of the place didn't disappoint either. Rich wood textures and colors, along with the stained-glass-looking light fixtures that hung over each table, created an inviting, homey atmosphere, totally reminiscent of the theme song's decree that "everybody knows your name."

We all got a big kick out of reading the menu. Gwen ordered *Frasier's Grilled Chicken Panini,* and Luke and I both had *Sam's Turkey Sandwich.* And for dessert, we split Boston Crème Pie.

After lingering at lunch for almost two hours, we made our way back to the car, heading in the direction of Mass General.

***

The hospital was huge, which I anticipated, since it's one of the top ranking medical facilities in the country. The large, white front section looked almost stately, sandwiched between the darker structures on either side. I tried to focus on the appearance of the building, the size, anything except the fact that I'd been born here.

It was just too weird to think about.

Inside, we navigated the hallways, dodging the steady stream of nurses, doctors, and visitors who also filled the halls. Gwen had called Brooke earlier in the week and arranged everything. She'd agreed to meet us at the hospital coffee shop during her afternoon break.

Coffee Central was in the main lobby of the Gray Building, and a woman sitting alone at a table for four noticed us immediately.

"Gwen Ellis?" she asked, standing up to greet us.

After the introductions and polite hellos, we sat down to talk.

"We appreciate you taking the time to talk with us," Gwen said, stirring half-and-half into her coffee.

"I hope you didn't make a special trip," Brooke replied. "I usually make it up to Camden once every couple of months."

Luke and I looked at each other, both thinking the same thing. We didn't have two months.

"We made a day of it," Gwen said. "Lucas is planning to run the BAA 5K in the spring, so we took a look at the route, then decided to show Layla a bit of Boston."

"That's nice." Brooke smiled at me, then looked at Lucas. "You're quite the runner, I've heard."

Luke just shrugged. "I enjoy it."

"You mentioned some family research that might somehow overlap with mine?" Brooke asked, looking back at Gwen.

"That's right. But Lucas is the one who's been researching, so I'll let him tell you about it."

"Basically I've discovered a connection between my family and the Emersons who own the antique store on Old Birch Lane."

Brooke nodded in recognition, and Lucas went on, leaving out lots of things that no one else needed to know. "I ran across a name in Arthur Emerson's will that I recognized from some of my mom's records. Amelia Cutler."

Brooke smiled. "My great-grandmother."

Luke went on. "Then we spoke with Patsy Emerson in Camden, and she told us about you."

"Our family scattered so much," Brooke said. "I wish we'd managed to stay closer to the ones who are still around, like William and Patsy."

"Life gets in the way of things sometimes," Gwen offered.

"Patsy also told us you knew something about what might've happened to Leo Emerson and his wife. Some tragic story." Beneath the table, Luke reached for my hand. "I was wondering if you could tell us about that."

"The story changed a lot over the years, or so my mom said," Brooke replied, her smile reaching the blue eyes that matched her scrubs. "I'm sure it was embellished and exaggerated, but I suppose that's what makes folklore memorable."

"Folklore makes for an interesting addition to bland genealogy charts," Gwen said.

"True." Brooke scooted her chair closer to the table, leaned across in order to talk softer. "Leo was accused of murdering a girl he had courted before he and Lillian married. She had apparently caused them no end of trouble, and her jealousy had become quite the thorn in their sides. Her body was found, partially naked and stabbed to death, on the banks of the creek behind Leo and Lillian's home. The townspeople immediately accused Leo. Nothing in the story suggests there was any evidence incriminating him, but in those days justice wasn't always rational. There wasn't much chance that Leo would be found innocent, so he and Lillian disappeared."

"Disappeared?" Luke and I said in unison. We knew very well that the two of them hardly just skipped town.

My hand felt clammy against Luke's and my pulse picked up.

"That's the story," Brooke shrugged. "Leo and Lillian fled the town to escape being punished for the murder. But personally, I've never believed Leo was guilty."

"And why is that?" Gwen asked, her voice cool and calm. I wondered how she did that when Luke and I were just about to crawl out of our skin.

"My mother always doubted the stories she'd heard from her great-aunts. She said they were terrible gossips, and delighted in telling the gruesome tale of how Leo murdered his former love interest. She much preferred the story she heard from her great-grandmother. She was twelve years old when Leo and Lillian disappeared, and she believed Leo to be as kind and good as a man could possibly be, and she firmly believed he'd been wrongly accused. She always said that if he'd run from the law, it was because the law was wrong."

"Wow," Lucas said, clearing his throat. "Quite the family story."

"Oh, here's something interesting for your family records." Brooke's eyes lit up, remembering. "My mother said her great-grandmother was fond of a little poem Leo's wife used to recite," Brooke said. *"Think you your acts will bring you joy. But hate and malice you employ. For the things you want you'll always yearn. Until the day you finally learn."*

Luke nudged my arm with his elbow, and I knew exactly what he meant. Picking up a pen, I opened my notebook and began jotting down the words to the poem.

"Maybe I've overly romanticized the entire tale," Brooke continued, "but I like to think those words have some meaning within the story."

"Perhaps you're right." Gwen reached across the table and patted Brooke's hand. "Thanks so much for taking the time to talk to us. All of this will make for great additions to Luke's research."

"It wasn't any trouble," Brooke said. "And I hope you're enjoying seeing the city, Layla, although you're not seeing much of it here."

"I bet people from all over come here," I said. Figuring I had nothing to lose and the potential to gain monumental information, I decided to go on. "I was born in this hospital."

Brooke looked puzzled. "I thought you moved to Sky Cove from Tennessee this summer."

"I did." I took a deep breath and felt Luke's arm come around my shoulder, a silent show of support. "I was adopted."

For part of a moment, everyone sat silent, and I could see the wheels turning in Brooke's mind.

"How old are you?" she asked.

"Sixteen. I'll be seventeen in January." I held my breath, torn between hoping she had information about my birth and wishing I didn't need to know.

"Strange," Brooke said, talking more to herself than to any of us. "Could it be?"

I waited to speak until she looked at me. "Do you know something about my birth mother?" Her eyes locked on mine and had it not been for Lucas's touch, I would've sworn Brooke and I were the only two people in the room.

"I'm not exactly sure," she said. "And I probably shouldn't say anything. I didn't work here at the time. Not to mention that adoption records are confidential for a reason. The information is very personal."

"Ms. McKenna," I began, leaning forward in order to speak more directly to her. "I've always known I was adopted. My parents have been open about it my entire life. I've never had the desire to seek out my birth parents, and in many ways I still don't. But Luke's research into his family history has given us reason to believe that our two families might be connected somehow, which is, of course, a surprise. If you have information that could help us confirm that, it would be very helpful."

Brooke looked from Lucas to me and back again. She probably thought we feared we might be cousins or something, which would put a big kibosh on our dating situation.

Perhaps that's why she decided to be forthcoming. "It's just so strange. Before she married Leo, Lillian's last name was Bostridge. Seventeen years ago, I was still living in Sky Cove, working for a doctor in Camden, and sometime in September of that year, one of the local high school girls, who's last name was also Bostridge, left town for a few months. The story was that her parents disapproved of her older boyfriend so they sent her to spend some time with relatives in Boston. I've always tried not to pay too much attention to the rumor mill, but Sky Cove is a small community, and word spread that the real reason she'd left for Boston was because she was pregnant."

"Did the rumor turn out to be true?" I asked, the shaking in my voice mimicking the trembling inside me.

Brooke shook her head. "No one ever knew for sure. But she came back to town in March, re-enrolled in Sky Cove Senior High, and went on to graduate two years later."

"You said her name was Bostridge. Do you know anything else about her?"

"That's the truly strange part," Brooke said. "I have no idea if she's related to Lillian's family or not, and I hadn't even realized the irony of the names until this moment."

"What irony?" I asked.

"The girl's name was Ashley Bostridge, and in May of this year, she married Seth Emerson, of Emerson's House of Antiques."

My stomach dropped. My heart pounded furiously, and sweat beaded on my forehead. Tears welled in my eyes, but I refused to let them spill. Information swirled in my head so quickly that I couldn't make sense of it all.

Ashley Emerson - with the dark auburn hair and the bright green eyes - was my birth mother. It didn't matter that we didn't have confirmation or DNA proof or anything else. I knew it was true.

Hadn't I felt that strange sense of recognition the first time I met her?

And there it was. The second intersecting event. The two families - Bostridge and Emerson - connecting once again when Ashley married Seth.

My brain pounded, trying to process the information that my heart refused to acknowledge. Luke's hand gripping mine, and his arm squeezing my shoulders brought me back to reality.

"Thank you," I whispered. "And I promise to treat this information with the utmost discretion."

Luke, Gwen, and I stood. The two them of said their goodbyes to Brooke McKenna while I silently walked across the hospital cafeteria.

A bulldozer might as well have just plowed me down. It couldn't feel anymore bewildering or painful than this. The logical side of my brain knew that the information about my birth was important to the journey Lucas and I were on. But the emotional side of me wanted no part of it, and I felt overwhelming sadness by the thought that I'd somehow betrayed my mom and dad by uncovering what had to be the identity of my birth mother.

Putting one foot in front of the other became almost impossible.

Then Luke took my hand and leaned down to kiss my cheek. "Let's just go. We'll talk about it later."

I appreciated the silence that Lucas and Gwen afforded me, but thirty minutes into the car ride home, I felt like talking.

"I guess we know the other intersecting event now," I said.

"Yeah." Luke shifted toward me in the back seat. "Ashley and Seth got married in May and you came to Sky cove in July."

"It's too much to just be coincidence." Gwen spoke from the driver's seat. "I imagine the two families connecting again through marriage was a powerful force. And with the two of you, apparently both descendants of these families, now in close proximity and involved with each other..." her voice trailed off.

I stared out the window.

"Layla, I'm so sorry," Luke whispered. "I know you feel awful, and I feel so bad about it."

I shook my head. "It's not your fault, Luke."

"Maybe I'm not responsible, but I still feel guilty."

"I know." I looked at him and managed a half-smile. "Just like I know I shouldn't feel like I've done something awful to my parents by figuring out who my birth mother is, but I still feel lousy about it."

"I wish things were different," he said.

"Michelle Bradford is my mother." Saying it out loud seemed to remind me of the fact that no matter who'd given birth to me, the people who'd raised me were my parents. And though I knew it would take some time before I felt okay about it all, I also knew that nothing would ever change the way I felt about my mom and dad.

"Besides," I continued. "There's more to be concerned about than just me feeling rotten. After what we saw in the last dream, you're going to need to be careful and not be around Kara at all. If we're right, and Leo was falsely accused of harming his old girlfriend, you've got to take extra precautions."

He nodded in agreement. "Next week is full anyway. State cross-country is a week from today, so there's a rigid practice schedule all week long. Plus, we have the Tolstoy test coming up, and I have two papers due pretty soon. And any free time I have is for you."

CHAPTER FORTY

Mom, Dad, and I had just finished Sunday lunch when my cell phone buzzed in my pocket. The caller ID told me it was Lucas. I answered as I headed upstairs toward my room.

"Hey Luke."

"How are you?"

He'd been so concerned about me yesterday. Finding out that Ashley Emerson was my birth mother had been a shock, and I still hadn't been able to reconcile that knowledge with my deep love for my parents.

But I would.

"I'm fine." I stepped into my bedroom and pushed the door shut behind me.

"I wanted to call last night, but I knew you'd be with your parents."

Sitting cross-legged on my bed, I heard the question he hadn't asked. He wanted to know if it had been odd or awkward being with them after what we'd learned in Boston.

"It wasn't weird," I said. "I thought it would be hard to interact with Mom and Dad normally, but it wasn't. The minute I walked in the house, everything was familiar and right."

"I'm glad," he said. "I was worried about you." "I guess my brain sort of compartmentalized everything. It's like I have this bit of knowledge tucked away and it's not allowed to affect anything else."

I didn't have to do anything with the information I'd uncovered. My parents didn't have to know. Ashley Emerson didn't have to know. I could file it away for later, and when I was older, I could petition the court in Tennessee to unseal my records.

But only if I chose to.

Knowing I had the choice was both comforting and empowering.

"Do you think you have a compartment left for something else?" he asked. "Because I have an idea."

"You do?" I asked, intrigued.

"I thought maybe if we went down to the beach, maybe we could somehow talk to them, or get them to talk to us."

It was an idea. One worth thinking about. I wondered why we hadn't thought to try it before. "You mean like when we asked them to show us things in our dreams?"

"Sort of." I heard him take a deep breath. "We know they were married. We know he was accused of killing his former girlfriend. We know the two of them tried to run away, but they found him and killed him before they could. We saw her die in childbirth sometime after he was killed. We need to know how to keep all this tragedy from happening again."

"Do you think they'll show us who he is?"

"I don't know," he said. "But it won't hurt to ask. And if they don't show us who he is, maybe we'll get some kind of clue about how to stop him."

As much as I didn't want to deal with all this after yesterday's revelations, I knew we had to. Something inside me told me this was quickly coming to a head. We needed to be ready.

I did not intend to lose Lucas this time.

At least not to a crazy person.

"When do you want to meet?"

**

We spread the blanket on the rocky sand near the outcropping. I thought it would feel eerie, being here, for the sole purpose of contacting Leo and Lillian, but to my surprise, it felt almost reassuring.

Without a word, Luke laid back on the blanket and held out his arms. I snuggled close, the warmth of him wrapping around me and permeating the heavy jacket I wore.

"Ready?" he whispered.

"Ready," I answered.

"Okay then." His arms tightened around me, and I nestled my head on his shoulder. "Show us what you got."

For a moment, I drifted along on the pure pleasure of being in Luke's embrace. Other than the fact that we were trying to connect with our dead past-selves, the situation was wildly romantic.

I couldn't be sure when the present and past merged together, but one moment I was cuddled with Luke, and the next, we sat on the blanket, across from Leo and Lillian.

They looked like us, only slightly older. It was sort of like looking into a mirror that morphed us into young twenty-somethings.

Damp fog rolled off the water, swirling around us, shrouding us in its heavy curtain until it seemed we floated on clouds.

There were no introductions, no pleasantries. I guessed after everything the four of us had been through together, everything they'd shared with us, regular niceties weren't necessary.

"I had courted Katherine," Leo's voice began. "Not with much seriousness, as we were both young, but enough that folks began to expect we would marry."

In the dream, Lucas took my hand, while Leo went on. I felt the warmth as his fingers slid against mine.

"In truth, I had no intention of marrying Katherine. I had no real knowledge of love and no desire to wed, but I knew enough to realize that I felt none for her. Lillian and her family came to town a few months later." Leo smiled, his mind in a far away memory. "I was smitten immediately. I like to think Lillian was as well."

"I was." Lillian's voice came a split second later. "Much to Katherine's dismay. She was jealous, of course, but it amounted to nothing but pettiness."

A soft look passed between them, and my heart warmed. I let myself imagine for a moment that years from now Lucas and I would look at each other like that.

Leo spoke next. "Carter took her jealousy, combined it with his own, and twisted it into something vile and evil."

"Carter?" Luke asked.

"Carter Johnston was a local man who took a liking to me," Lillian said. "I hadn't noticed him, nor was I aware of his interest."

"He knew of Katherine's jealousy and convinced her to help him come between us." Leo slipped his arm around Lillian and pulled her close. "When we married and it became clear that nothing Katherine did would succeed in separating us, the madness took him."

"Carter devised a plan to get rid of Leo, as well as cover up his conspiracy with Katherine," Lillian said. "He killed her, brutally, and left her by the creek near our home where he knew we would find her. Then he told the townspeople that Leo was the murderer. Made them believe he'd killed her in a rage."

"They came for me that night," Leo continued. "I knew they would. The menfolk were livid and seeking justice. I knew they would not listen to me. I tried to leave in time to escape. Lillian and I were to meet at the sea and run away. But Carter anticipated what we'd planned, and when Lillian came to the beach to find me, it was too late."

The fear and sorrow I felt at the memory of what had happened on the beach was mirrored in Lillian's eyes. My heart ached for her, because unlike me, she hadn't been able to wake up and realize it had all been a dream.

"Carter and his men found me," Lillian said, her expression full of sorrow. "I'd collapsed in the sand, caring not what might happen to me. I was hardly even aware of being carried away. I'm sure I lost consciousness, because the next memory I have was of being inside a strange house. Carter was there, prattling on about how everything would be fine now that I was with him. He said I didn't have to be afraid of Leo anymore and that he would take care of me. I believe he'd actually deluded himself into believing the lies he spewed."

"But you got away from him at some point, didn't you?" I asked, remembering the awful scene where she'd died alone in a shack.

Lillian nodded. "I'm not certain how many days passed while I was inside Carter's house, but I refused to speak or interact. He left food and water for me, and continued to talk incessantly about how my state of mind would improve once I purged myself of memories of Leo. There were times I was afraid he would force himself upon me, but thankfully he did not."

Luke's hand tightened around mine. "I'm really glad to know that," he said.

"I realized I was with child, though it wasn't visible to Carter yet. I knew I had to get away, that the only hope my child had was if I could escape from Carter's evil. The next time he left to go to the water pump, I fled through the back door. I knew it would take him several minutes to retrieve the water, so I crept quietly for a moment, putting distance between the cabin and myself. Then I ran. I hid in the woods that night, frightened and alone, but so thankful to be away from him. I had no idea where I was, what direction I was moving, but eventually, I came upon a deserted shack. There was a stream close by, and a farmhouse and barn within an easy walk. I knew I shouldn't steal, but I had no choice. I took what I needed from the barn in order to build a fire. Occasionally I would take an egg or two from the chicken coop. I managed to keep myself fed well enough for a while."

Tears formed in my eyes and I did not try to stop them. I knew what came next.

"The baby came early," Lillian continued. Leo's expression hardened, the sadness for all that had happened etched on his forever-young face. "I was young and had no idea about childbirth, but I knew something was wrong. It was as if someone set fire to my womb."

I remembered exactly. I'd felt the fire in my own body the night I'd watched her die.

"He killed us all," Leo said. "Me, Lillian, and our child. And for what? He did not succeed in keeping Lillian for himself, and once we were gone he failed at everything he put his hand to. His farm, a mercantile, eventually a marriage. All of them ended badly. He ended up on the wrong side of a fight with a drunken man one summer night and died as a result."

Knowing that Leo and Lillian had watched Carter reap what he'd sown gave me some satisfaction. In no way was it punishment enough, but at least he hadn't gone on to live happily ever after.

"Don't let him separate you," Lillian said. "If the two of you can weather this storm, our deaths will not have been in vain."

"How?" Luke and I asked in unison.

"He must remember," Lillian said. "He must know he cannot succeed. *Think you your acts will bring you joy. But hate and malice you employ. For the things you want you'll always yearn. Until the day you finally learn.*"

Sad smiles crossed their faces an instant before their bodies turned translucent. Though the visual connection faded, I could still feel the strength of our bond in my heart. Part of me wished we could keep them here.

In the next moment, my eyes fluttered open, my head still against Luke's shoulder. I felt him shift, his hand brushing my hair with light strokes. The sun sat high in the sky, indicating that Sunday afternoon was still young. I wondered how long we'd been asleep.

Lucas pressed a light kiss against my lips as we sat up. "Now we have the whole story. Details and all."

I nodded. "What happened to them was so horrible. It makes Vaseline on my windshield look like nothing."

"Whatever happens, we stay together," he said. "If he can't succeed in splitting us up, maybe the cycle will be broken."

And wasn't that just the way I wanted to keep Lucas in my life? Out of some kind of obligation to our past-selves? It was almost worse than thinking his feelings for me weren't real, but rather just "left-overs".

But he was right. Whoever was targeting us couldn't succeed. It was time to put an end to the madness that had taken over Leo and Lillian's life.

CHAPTER FORTY-ONE

The next week rolled by without incident.

Luke and I stayed together – or in contact – the majority of the time. We'd even resorted to texting each other between every class. The only time we went any length of time without talking or texting was during cross-country practice.

Tolstoy proved to be a harder test than Frost, but Luke and I both felt pretty confident about the test we'd taken yesterday.

On Friday afternoon, I hung around in the parking lot after school, waiting to see Lucas and the rest of the runners off as they ran their last practice round before the state meet tomorrow. Typical of Friday afternoons with no home football game to look forward to, several crowds of kids loitered, making their plans for the night.

Jessie stood next to me, leaned against my car, the brisk November wind breezing around us. Mr. Hartley had scheduled a chemistry test for Monday of all days, so Jessie and I were studying this afternoon.

After all, tomorrow was the state cross-country meet and I would be driving back up to Belfast to cheer Luke and the other guys on. There would be no studying tomorrow.

We watched the runners take off from behind the school locker room, setting out on their practice course.

Luke looked back toward my car, waving when he saw Jessie and me. I gave him a big thumbs up and a smile.

"He looks really happy," Jessie said.

I smiled, and knew without looking at my reflection that it was a really huge, stupid grin.

"But if we're going to get finished studying in time for you to see your man after he runs," Jessie continued, with a friendly shoulder bump, "we better get started."

With a laugh, we got in our cars and headed to my house for an afternoon of chemistry punishment.

***

My cell phone buzzed just as Jessie was backing out of my driveway. I waved goodbye to her as I reached in my pocket.

Smiling, I flipped the phone open to read a text message from Lucas.

Meet me on the beach.

U know the spot.

Surprise!

Strange, but okay. We hadn't made a point of avoiding the beach, and the memories we'd made there hadn't all been bad. I figured it would be a shame to let such a beautiful spot become a place we avoided.

I went in the house long enough to grab my coat and backpack, and tell my mom where I was headed, then hopped behind the wheel and took off.

***

I arrived before Lucas, and walked toward the outcropping. I felt connected to him here, tied to him by what had happened in the past and what we had experienced in the present. Leo's death. Lillian's abduction. Our first kiss. The communication we'd experienced here with Leo and

Lillian. And despite all that had been done to us in this place, the beauty of it still drew me in, and I longed for our good memories to outweigh the bad.

Closing my eyes and breathing the salty sea air, I imagined the potential happier moments Lucas and I could create here.

In my hand, my phone vibrated. Expecting Lucas, I answered without looking at the screen.

"Hello."

It was Jessie. "Ohmigosh, did you hear?"

"Hear what?" The alarm in her voice worried me.

"Something happened to Kara."

My stomach dropped. "What?"

"I'm not sure." She took a deep breath and went on. "I went back to school to get my history notes out of the locker, and everyone was talking about it. Someone found Kara down by the creek, near where the cross-country people were running. She'd been beaten up. Someone said she might've also been drugged."

Everything in me trembled. My knees threatened to crumble beneath me.

I didn't have to wonder what came next.

"Layla," Jessie continued. "Corey and Will came back to school to get their stuff from the locker room, and they told me that the police are talking to Lucas."

Even knowing it ahead of time didn't take the sting out of hearing it.

"No," I whispered, more to myself than to Jessie. "No, no, no, no."

"He couldn't have done it," Jessie assured me. "No way would Lucas do anything like that. I'm sure it's just a misunderstanding."

I ordered myself to think. If Luke was being questioned by the police, how did he manage to send me a text fifteen minutes ago?

And then Jessie's words fell into place.

Luke didn't send me that text.

"I have to go, Jessie." I dug frantically in my coat pocket for my keys, hoping I wasn't too late. "I have to get there."

I didn't wait for her to respond before I flipped my phone shut.

I turned around, prepared to sprint back up the beach to my car, and nearly plowed him over.

"Corey."

CHAPTER FORTY-TWO

Dear Lord. It was Corey.

"I figured you'd heard about Lucas by now," he said, his eyes so empty I barely recognized him.

I nodded, thinking that the best chance I had to get out of here was to pretend I had no idea he was behind it.

"Jessie just called," I said, forcing a smile. "It was nice of you to come find me, though. I should hurry and get back to town."

I started to step away, but he stepped, too, and blocked my way. My head still reeled from the knowledge that Corey was behind all of this. Luke's best friend had been the one to betray him and set him up.

Fate, destiny, or whatever you want to call her, it was a cruel, nasty bitch.

"I don't think you're going to be able to help him." He touched my face and bile rose up and burned my throat.

"Maybe not," I shrugged. "But I could at least be there."

He narrowed his eyes. And the words started falling, swirling in my mind, senseless and random.

Focus, I ordered myself. If this didn't end today, the next attack would be on Lucas. I could not let that happen.

I had to let his thoughts in, had to see what was going on in his mind. Maybe, just maybe, it would give me an advantage.

Always, always trying to protect him.

Once I let them start, the words came, unfiltered

Never once looking anywhere but him. You'll look at me, though. It won't be long now, my love. You belong to me. No matter what I have to do. I won't lose, not this time. Even if I have to kill him.

His face hardened, and Corey seemed a million miles away. As if his body was now occupied by Carter Johnston.

Could it be? Was Corey Jacobs really locked away somewhere inside. Had Carter taken him over completely?

And did it even matter?

I decided to take a chance.

"Carter?"

His eyes darted toward me, fixing on my face. "Lillian."

Fear coursed through me with a force that matched the waves crashing on the shore, and I trembled violently inside. I said nothing as he stepped toward me.

"I knew you would see the truth," he said. His voice no longer resembled Corey's. "After all these years, you see it. I am the one for you."

I shook my head. "Carter, you know this doesn't end well. It never will."

His thoughts jumbled, melded into a confusing mix of past and present, as he fought the memories that would prove I was telling the truth. He shook his head, forcing his mind back to the delusion that he'd lived in so long. The delusion that allowed him to believe the two of us belonged together.

"As soon as he's gone, everything will be fine. We'll be happy." He grabbed my hand, hard enough to be uncomfortable, and pulled me along the shore, away from the outcropping.

The wind off the ocean lifted my hair off my neck, blowing it wildly around my face, bits of the cold slipping between my sweater and the skin on my neck.

All around me, inside me, chaos swirled, from the wind, to the fear, and to Carter's delusions.

I must get her away from here, far enough away that she forgets.

As his thoughts scrolled across my consciousness, I sensed his confusion, his frustration. Lillian hadn't fought him before. With Leo already dead, she'd had no fight left. But now, having known the truth about the past, my resistance threw a wrench in his plans.

I pulled against his hold, digging my feet in the wet sand, making him turn to face me. "Carter, Lillian didn't go with you because she wanted to. You killed her will to live when you killed Leo. And later, she ran away from you because she hated you and everything you'd done."

"No! No!" His grip on my arm tightened, enough that I knew there would be a bruise, and the confusion in his eyes morphed into anger.

The surf pounded harder as the wind whipped with more force. I had to shout to be heard above it. "Lillian didn't love you, and neither do I!"

For a moment, I thought he would hit me. His face iced with a fury far colder than the November air.

The sadness that came next scared me even more.

Then it must be death.

He changed directions, and instead of pulling me along beside the water, he waded in, forcing me to trail behind him.

The frigid water soaked through my socks and the bottom of my jeans. Fear masked what was surely an almost burning cold against my feet.

I realized then that he meant to kill us both. That if I couldn't love him, he wouldn't allow me to love Lucas. Hot anger surged through me, canceling the cold that would've otherwise taken my breath. And I let the anger explode, unleashing it at him.

"Stop it Corey! Or Carter, or whoever the hell you are!" Screaming, I jerked my arm out of his grasp. Rage burned inside me. Never had I felt such loathing. "You killed Leo and it accomplished nothing! Lillian didn't love you. She *never* would've loved you. You might as well have killed her with your own hands."

He lunged for me again and I jumped to the side, stumbling in the surf but successfully dodging him. His thoughts streamed in so fast I couldn't comprehend them, nor did I want to. I knew he was incensed by the look on his face and I did not care. If he thought he was pissed off now, he hadn't seen anything yet.

"You may think you own me," I yelled. "You may think you own this place. You may think you're entitled to have whatever you want. Bullshit! This is my life, Carter Johnston or Corey Jacobs or whatever name you want to go by. This place, this time, it's mine and Luke's. This time you don't get to win, because we won't let you!"

His eyes darted back and forth, the expression shifting from hatred to sadness with each movement. I was no psychiatrist, but I could tell that Corey and Carter were battling for control.

Then he was still. His eyes lifted to mine, empty and malicious, and I knew that Corey had lost.

And then, in a last ditch effort, I repeated the words Lillian had spoken. "Think you your acts will bring you joy. But hate and malice you employ. For the things you want you'll always yearn. Until the day you finally learn."

His eyes lit with flames of hatred.

"You belong to me," he uttered, in a voice that was not Corey's.

CHAPTER FORTY-THREE

Pain sliced through my skull as he grabbed me by the hair, wrenching my head against his chest until his arm came around me in a headlock. I struggled, flailing wildly while he pulled me further into the water. The freezing water crept up to my chest, my clothes pulled against me like quicksand.

Something caught my eye. A blur, as if something was moving far up the beach toward the parking area. If someone was there, all I needed was a distraction, a split second to get out of his hold and run screaming toward the movement.

With strength I did not think I possessed, I jabbed my elbow hard into his ribs. When he jerked from the impact, I swung upward, my fist connecting with what I hoped was his nose.

Take that you sorry piece of shit.

Stunned, his grip around my neck loosened and I sprung away from him, just in time see him knocked back toward the sand by Lucas, moving faster than any human should be able to.

Then it clicked. The blur I'd seen. Luke's gifting.

Corey stood up, dripping wet from having landed in the shallow water, only to be launched into the air again when Luke's fist slammed into his chin.

"Layla!" Luke shouted, running back toward me.

He threw his arms around me, hugging me tight and lifting me out of the water at the same time.

Back on the sand, I saw a bewildered Corey lying on the ground, not offering to fight back or run away. Did he really have no idea what had just happened?

Luke sat me back on my feet, but didn't let go. His eyes searched my face, frantic, as his arms tightened around me again.

I answered his unspoken question. "I'm not hurt."

He nodded, pulling me flush against him and pressing his lips against my forehead.

Police sirens sounded in the distance.

"Kara?" I asked. "Is she hurt badly?"

"One of the cops that was questioning me got a call from the hospital that she was awake and talking."

The sirens got closer.

"Are the police looking for you?"

He shrugged. "Not sure. Don't really care."

Corey moaned and sat up. "What the - "

"Shut up and don't move," Luke snapped.

"What happened, Luke?" I asked.

"All of us took off running," he said. "The track that winds down behind Emerson House. Right after we started, Corey said he forgot something and headed back to the locker room. We all went on. I was about to finish up the run, and when I came around the curve that leads back to school a cop stopped me. Hauled me down to the station in the freaking squad car. Told me Kara'd supposedly gone to meet me down by the creek, because I'd texted her and told her to. Now she was beaten up and drugged with something, and did I know anything about it. It all clicked then. Corey borrowed my cell phone during sixth period."

"That explains the text I got from you, telling me to meet you here. He must've done it when he went back to the locker room." I looked over to Corey, still sitting on the sand, wondering if he was listening to all of this.

"I put the pieces together, and I knew in my gut somehow he'd get you here." He pulled off my soaked jacket and threw it to the ground. "Here," he said, unzipping his hoodie. "Take this. You're freezing."

I didn't argue. His sweatshirt, dry and warm from being on his body, did a lot to relieve the nasty cold.

"As soon as I heard the cop on the phone with the hospital, I got up and left. I figured they'd find me if they wanted to hound me some more. Jessie was coming into the station as I was running out. I told her to tell the officer if he wanted me, he'd find me down at the beach."

Now out of their cars and headed toward us, the police guys didn't look happy.

Corey stood up. "Luke, I got no idea – "

Lucas cut him off again. "No idea why you were dragging Layla into the freezing ocean trying to drown her? Or no idea why you beat Kara, fed her some drug to knock her out, then blamed me for it?"

"Oh my God," Corey whispered. The little bit of color left in his face drained, leaving him white as a sheet. Realization dawned in his eyes, defeat and confusion playing across his expression.

The two police officers reached us, and one of them clasped Corey on the shoulder. "Corey Jacobs, we need to talk to you down at the station. Your folks are already on their way."

"I don't understand any of this." Corey's voice shook. "I don't understand how any of it happened."

"I think he's been hallucinating," Luke offered. "Maybe he's taking the drugs he gave to Kara."

"We'll do the investigating, son," the taller officer said. "You two just stay in town so we can take your statements."

***

"I think he may have been on some kind of drug," Lucas said to my mother, who sat next to him on the sofa.

He'd followed me home and insisted on explaining things to my parents himself.

"And he did all this because he was jealous that you're dating my daughter?" my dad asked from across the room. We'd left the reincarnation part out, as well as the part about Corey/Carter wanting to kill himself and drag me along with him.

"Apparently, sir," Luke nodded. "I don't know how I didn't see it. I don't think I'll ever forgive myself for putting Layla through that."

"You didn't put me through anything," I insisted.

Despite everything, Lucas still felt guilty and somehow responsible.

"She's right." Mom put her arm around Luke's shoulder. "In fact, you got Layla away from him before something awful happened."

"The most important thing is that it's over," Dad said. "Kara Jennings is all right, and this kid is going to get the help he needs."

"I hope you all will still allow me to see Layla," Luke said to my parents. Then he looked at me. "And that you'll still want to see me."

Oh good grief. Was he really *that* oblivious? I still wondered what his feelings would be once things settled down and the past – hopefully - stopped creeping in on us, but did he really think I was just done with him now?

"Of course," Mom reassured him.

Dad nodded his agreement.

Lucas took my hand.

I just smiled.

And he smiled back.

***

Understandably, my parents wanted to re-negotiate the State Cross Country Meet the following day, which prior to the events of the day before, I'd had permission to drive myself to.

I didn't argue, even though the meet was only an hour away in Belfast.

Gwen was already scheduled to ride on the team bus as a chaperone, so Dad left the shop in the hands of Charlie, his assistant manager, and he and mom drove me.

I found their over-protectiveness very sweet, under the circumstances. I think they also realized just how serious things were between Luke and me. It was nice that they were taking an interest in him and the things that were important to him.

And it was very cool for Mom, Dad, Gwen, and I to all be there to see Luke cross the finish line first and with the state title in his division.

The smile on my face at that moment had its roots deep in my heart.

CHAPTER FORTY-FOUR

Back at school on Monday, the business with Corey and Kara was all the talk. Luke had been cleared of all wrongdoing when Kara told the police it was Corey who'd met her at the creek, given her a drugged bottle of water, and then once she'd begun to feel light-headed, hit her several times and knocked her out.

His plan had not been well thought out. He obviously hadn't meant to kill Kara, as Carter had killed Katherine, which in turn left her able to tell the truth about what had been done to her and by whom.

I supposed it was a risk past-souls took when they reincarnated into teenagers. Thankfully Lucas and I had been able to sort through the images and information and discover the truth that allowed Leo and Lillian to finally rest.

I'd thought all along that the intrigue of what we'd experienced would make regular, high-school stuff - like classes, tests, ballgames, and gossip - seem mundane and ordinary.

On the contrary.

I was glad to get back to *normal* and *boring*.

Luke insisted on picking me up on Monday so that we arrived at school together, and when we walked into the lobby, I felt all the excitement and nervousness I'd felt on the first day of school.

The prospect of taking notes in chemistry actually appealed. The thought of lugging my backpack from class to class didn't seem like a chore.

And I still felt a tad bit uncomfortable in the spotlight.

Which was exactly where we were when we stepped into the building.

There were hugs and pats on the back, and a lot of "glad you're okay" sentiments. Luke and I just smiled and said thanks to everyone. We both knew the limelight would be over soon.

When the warning bell rang, Kara approached us, followed by, Erika and Tina, the same girls who forever trailed along behind her.

She sported a multi-colored shiner on one eye, and a nasty bruise across the other cheek. I was surprised she'd come to school in less-than-perfect condition.

Luke nodded in greeting. "Kara."

She looked from him to me, then back again.

"I'm just here to pick up my assignments for the next few days. I thought about sending my mom in to pick them up, so no one would see me," she said. "But I decided I didn't want to cover up what happened. People should know the truth."

"Brave of you," Luke said. "And I agree."

"I know what you went through was terrible, Kara," I said. "But I'm really glad you weren't seriously hurt."

She acknowledged me with a shrug, adjusted the strap of her purse, then looked back at Lucas.

"I'm sorry about the prom pictures and the sign on Layla's locker," she whispered. "I went along with Corey's plans to try and split you and Layla up because I was jealous."

At least she was being honest, even if she couldn't apologize directly to me.

"I know," Luke said, not exactly letting her off the hook, but letting her know he wouldn't hold a grudge. "Let's just put the whole ordeal behind us."

"Okay," Kara replied, and with one last glance at Luke, she rejoined her friends before heading toward the front door.

Erika and Tina headed in the direction of their hallway, and looked back over their shoulders, giving me the same once over they always did. With a roll of their eyes they let me know that I still didn't measure up in their book.

And then it hit me. Somewhere along the way, I really had stopped caring what people like those girls thought. I'd always wanted to be indifferent, to let those kinds of judgments roll off me, but I'd never been quite able to get there.

Now I just felt sorry for them.

Because I knew the truth. They judged because they weren't comfortable in their own skin. They had no idea who they really were, and in order to make up for it, they cut other people down.

What a miserable way to live.

But I knew who I was.

I looked at Luke and smiled.

He kissed my forehead with a slight chuckle that said he knew some things never changed. "See you in lit class."

And off we went to start the day.

CHAPTER FORTY-FIVE

We were back at the beach. A month after the incident with Corey, our past seemed a million miles away.

And, so far, my fears that Luke's feelings would change once the mystery was solved had not come to fruition. With each day the doubts grew smaller. I felt as close to him as I ever had.

The rock outcropping held so much significance for the two of us, and no matter what, we just couldn't look at this place negatively. Even though the first time we'd been here together had been in response to a dream that scared us both, and despite the fact that Corey/Carter had tried to carry out his plan in this very spot, there had been moments here we could smile about.

Enough that we'd made the conscious decision to make good memories here. A brand new beginning in the place that had held such heartache in the past.

Starting today, in the cold, crisp morning air, as we watched the sun make its first appearance on the water.

"Does it feel weird being back here," Luke asked, reaching for my hand and lacing our gloved fingers together as we walked toward the rocks.

I shook my head. "It feels right. Like we've changed the history of this place. Maybe we haven't erased the bad stuff, but we've covered it up with good things."

He smiled. "Yeah. I agree."

White patches dotted the beach and topped the rocks of the outcropping, leftover from last week's snowfall. The wind would've been brutal had we not bundled up in heavy parkas, scarves, gloves, and toboggans.

Dealing with the cold might've seemed like a lot of work in order to have a walk on the beach, but for us, it was about more than just a romantic moment.

It was about creating our own history.

On the other side of the rocks, in the exact spot where, in that terrible dream, I'd watched Leo die, Luke pulled to a stop.

"I have an early Christmas present for you."

"Really?" Surprise bloomed in my heart, and a smile spread across my face.

Removing his gloves, he reached in his jacket pocket. He pulled out a tiny box, wrapped in silver foil paper and handed it to me.

"I thought it was appropriate."

"Appropriate?"

"Just open it, Layla," he laughed. "I want to watch your face when you see it."

I'd given some thought into Luke's Christmas present, but it seemed he'd beaten me to the punch with his pre-Christmas gift.

I tore the paper at the end of the box, pulling until it was completely off, and lifted the lid.

A silver necklace lay delicately on the white tissue paper inside. Picking it up, I noticed the green stone pendant. Silver wire wrapped around it in a whimsical pattern, criss-crossing the bright green color of the glass.

I realized it then, that this was the piece of sea glass I'd found the first time Luke and I came to the beach together. My heart expanded with joy and tears filled my eyes.

"Lucas," I whispered, looking up to find him smiling brilliantly.

"It's our good luck sea glass." He took the necklace from my hands, unclasped the hook, and stepped behind me to fasten it around my neck. Even against the dark brown of my parka, the green glass sparkled.

"It's beautiful," I said, reaching up to hold the stone in my hand. "I love it."

He noticed me looking down at it. "I wanted a long chain, so you'd be able to see it when you were wearing it."

"You had this made?"

He came back around in front of me and took my hands in his. "My mom knows a lady who makes jewelry from sea glass. I took it to her a couple of weeks ago."

"Thank you seems so inadequate," I said, holding the pendant once again. The necklace was exquisite and perfect, but even more perfect was the thought and sentiment that had gone into it.

Luke just grinned. "I love you, Layla."

My world tilted, narrowed, until the whole of my focus fixed on him. They were the words I'd wanted to hear... wanted to say... the words that had lived for so long in my heart.

I knew I should respond, give those words back to him, but when I tried all that made it past the lump in my throat was a surprised gasp.

Luke went right on. "I wanted to tell you in a way that acknowledged the past, but didn't dwell on it. From now on, it's just about us. About Luke and Layla. And we're together because we want to be, because we love each other."

I felt the tears start down my cheeks, the early December wind chilling them on my skin. Everything I'd feared, all the uncertainty I'd carried, just melted away in that moment.

Without even knowing, Lucas had put it all to rest.

"Am I right?" he asked, placing his palm against my cheek, wiping the tear with his thumb. "That we love each other?"

I burst out laughing, not because it was funny but because I was so incredibly happy.

"Yes," I managed, though the word was drawn out between giggles. "I love you, Lucas. I love you so much!"

I threw my arms around his neck, and his encircled my waist, as he lifted me off the ground and spun me in circles, laughing right along with me.

The sun shined like a ball of fire in the distance, sitting just on top of the sea. The brilliant light hit the edge of the outcropping, creating an almost blinding glow.

"Layla," Luke whispered, placing my feet back on the sand. "Look."

Looking toward the rocks, I saw them. Leo and Lillian.

They stood in the center of the light, hands clasped together, smiles on their faces.

And in Lillian's arms, a tiny, sleeping baby.

My heart swelled with happiness as Luke's arm came around my shoulders, hugging me tightly to him.

They looked peaceful, content, as if at last their past had finally been put to rest. I hoped their eternity together was as beautiful as this moment was for Luke and me.

As we watched, Leo bent his head to brush a kiss across Lillian's cheek, then kissed the forehead of the sweet child in her arms. When he straightened, his lips formed words that needed no sound in order for us to understand.

Thank you.

The light began to fade as the sun rose higher above the water, and Leo and Lillian waved to us as their images became translucent, finally disappearing from our view. We didn't say it out loud, but we knew it was the last time we would see them.

Luke turned to me and smiled, and love for him burned bright in my heart.

And there, on the same beach that had brought us together, between sweet, tender kisses and joyous laughter, we began *our* chapter of history.

THE END

COMING SOON
Once and For All

How nice that at least one person was not in the "Phoebe Campbell is a freak" club.

I liked Mr. Pierce, the guy who owned the hardware store. Apparently he was too old to realize I was the most uncool person in Sky Cove.

I crunched across the snowy mush in the hardware store parking lot. Typical Maine, the day before New Year's Eve was drab gray and bitter cold, but I didn't care.

I needed paint. And wood. And other artsy stuff.

I loved Christmas break. Not because I got all crazy with holiday spirit, but because it meant a break from the black hole known as Sky Cove Senior High School. It also meant loads of time spent in the little spare bedroom that my dad had let me turn into an art studio two years ago.

Head down, I did my best to shield myself against the biting wind, pushing toward the front door of Pierce Home Improvement. Winter in Maine always sucked, but the wind made today worse than usual. I was almost there, just about to step inside and out of the icebox, when the door opened and someone in a really nice pair of leather boots pounded out.

And straight into me.

My center of gravity already off from walking half bent over with my head lowered out of the wind, I lost my balance and tumbled back.

Right onto my butt.

And even through several layers of clothes and a heavy coat, the ground was wet and cold against my backside.

Great.

But it got worse.

Staring down at me was the dumb jock football star, at whose feet all of Sky Cove Senior High worshipped.

Todd Miller.

"Uh, Sorry," he said, but did nothing to help me up.

Like I needed his help.

I pushed up, gaining my feet without slipping again on the ice. The stupid moron just stood there looking at me.

"Watch where you're going," I snapped, and walked inside, leaving him standing there in the cold.

Twenty minutes later, I emerged from the store, a large bag of paint, wood, and other supplies dangling from one arm. A glance toward the near-empty parking lot told me that Todd Miller and his big, stupid truck were long gone.

Thank God for small favors.

At home, I went straight to work in my studio. I'd developed an idea for a shadow-box display of small wooden carvings depicting Maine wildlife. Getting accepted to college wasn't the problem for me, but paying for it would be. I had high hopes that I could pick up some scholarship money in the Coastal Maine Artists Guild student art competition.

Inspiration came quickly and pretty soon my hands took over, each subtractive action of my carving knife and V-tool bringing the figure further to life. The grain of the scrap maple hardwood Mr. Pierce had given me gave extra dimension to the little animal taking shape in my hands.

I wasn't sure how long I worked, but when I finished, I sat the small red fox on the table and leaned back to look.

And smiled.

It was so life like, so playful. As if I'd somehow captured its personality.

If I could create more like this, maybe a bear and a moose, the display would be spectacular.

My gaze narrowed, and my peripheral vision seemed to fall away, leaving only a small tunnel of sight that was trained on the small fox figurine. I wanted to blink, to shake my head and make my eyesight return to normal, but I could not take my eyes off the fox.

Then I wasn't looking at the figure anymore. In front of my eyes I saw what could only be the floor of a forest. Snow covered the ground, dotted with fallen leaves and twigs. Tree branches moved and creaked with the wind.

The forest was dark, as if I were seeing it exactly the way it would look at this precise moment, and all around me I heard the organic silence of the woods.

My heartbeat picked up and my breathing became rapid as fear surged through me. Fear of what I had no clue - the scene in front of me was benign enough – but I felt it nonetheless.

Lost. I felt lost. Completely enveloped in the unknown. Suffocated by the lack of reality.

What in the world was happening?

The sight of the forest was not unfamiliar, but somehow it felt totally foreign to me and I wanted desperately to escape.

The front door opened, and I heard my dad call my name. I blinked away the fog.

And I was looking at my tiny red fox again.

Crazy.

ABOUT THE AUTHOR

Amy Durham discovered her love of writing in the sixth grade. What began as a love of writing poetry soon turned into stories scribbled into school notebooks. In the eighth grade, her English teacher told her she was good at it and encouraged her to continue to put pen to paper. At that moment, the die was cast, and writing would forever be a part of her life.

As an adult, Amy focuses her efforts on writing Young Adult Fiction... adventure, romance, and life-lessons... woven together as imagination and escape for young readers. Amy holds a firm belief that books are not only entertaining, but have the ability to transform young lives. A book can educate. A book can teach compassion and kindness. A book can spark interest. A book can be a companion. Simply put, books can accompany and guide young readers as they try to navigate their way through the twisted, confusing roads of adolescence.

She lives in Kentucky, where she is a middle school teacher. She and her husband of 15 years are raising three wild, intelligent, and creative boys, giving her plenty of fodder for the love and adventure she enjoys putting in her stories!

Amy loves to hear from readers. You can contact her at:

amybdurham@gmail.com
amy-durham.blogspot.com
twitter.com/Amy_Durham
facebook.com/AuthorAmyDurham

www.ingramcontent.com/pod-product-compliance
Lightning Source LLC
Chambersburg PA
CBHW071311170626
46809CB00001B/401